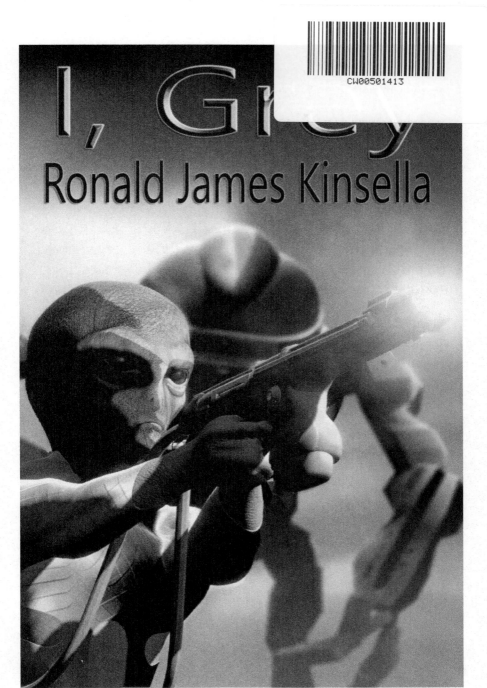

I, Grey

Ronald James Kinsella

I, GREY

Ronald Kinsella
(Illustrated by the author)

For my brother, Philip

Neil Geddes Ward – a smashing friend and adviser.

David and Jill Young – lovely souls.

And finally, for Sacha Christie and Frank Willis.

Report submitted to Galactic High Command for His Supreme Eminence, Zoltak Zan II
Name: Clone 21333 – AKA, Taffy

Monday – 7th July 2027
Arrival

I have been sent to Earth by Galactic High Command on a very important mission. My job is to locate an enemy of our race, a lizard by the name of Baltazar, and to basically kill him. The boss back home (which is Alpha Sector 3) wants proof of the execution, once the slippery toerag has been caught, and to film his ultimate demise. He vanished near the Earth in 1946. I've also been asked to investigate the disappearance of our guys dispatched here in 1947 and of whom never returned.

Galactic High Command

Consequently, they had an older ship compared to mine, but it was light-years ahead of anything the humans possessed. It is unlikely the primitives had efficient arsenal at the time to bring it down. Our team were seeking the rogue reptile. Whether he discovered the ploy and had them eliminated, or the group simply took a detour, is unclear. It is my job to accomplish this assignment as swiftly and effectively as possible. This is my journal of the events and of my own personal visit to the backward world inhabited by semi intelligent trolls. They're called humans, but personally I think they look appalling.

Arrival at this pretty-looking marble of a world has been satisfactory. This new saucer the Guv's supplied is nippy. Yes, it's small, but the responses on it are just incredible. It's streamline and can approach speeds beyond that of light. It also has an invisibility cloak, along with super cool weapons.

I took the liberty of testing them out whilst on approach to Earth, blasting one of its orbiting artificial tin-can thingies to smithereens and of which had something called 'VIRGIN' marked on its side. Goodness knows who 'VIRGIN' is but, in the human definition of the word, I guess it has never copulated.

There is a dense cloud covering this part of the world and, within no time at all, I am upon a vast superstructure of brick and metal towers spanning the horizon. I engage the invisibility cloak of the ship and have a good nosey around while gliding over this native tribe. Below, crisscrossing the immense chaos of primitive dwellings, I can see the trolls themselves, hectic about their little affairs.

So much smoke and noise! Operating the Super-Snooper, I can hear a chorus of utter garbage emanating from these hominids, and the noise is so deafening and disturbing, I mute the thing, before setting about landing. I want to get a feel for this place first before engaging the mission. Consulting my databanks, I swiftly discover that I am in a place called New York in the USA. Well, this is a good starting point, as my old pals who arrived in 1947 were last reported within this landmass. Also, Baltazar, the reptilian version of Hitler, and who fled his world after his true intentions were exposed, was last tracked here in his scaly ship. The dictator is wanted by the Draconian Royal Family for not only plotting to blow them up, but for also stealing their very latest star ship in his vigil to escape capture.

Approaching planet Earth

Incidentally, The Draconian Empire has put a bounty on his head and though we, The Greys, don't see eye-to-eye with them, we've reached a compromise in attempting to seek, locate and destroy the slippery snake. They also want proof of his demise.

Baltazar nearly caused World War 13 with us, wishing to have us enslaved and to serve The Draconian Empire, against the Royal Family's wishes. However, we managed to bust the greasy croc's arse and drove him back, along with his weak-minded army, though he was rallying for another attack before things turned very sour for him.

The transparent dome of my saucer gives a great view of the sky and metropolis. The older models were drab, with no open portholes. The crew just used boring old telepathy to view the outside world and, after much protest, our scientists upgraded the ships. Who likes just staring at bland metal? It's crazy, especially on long flights.

The cloud cover above is diminishing and there's a real nice sea of blue, with the troll's star beautifully visible. I guess this is what they call morning. Earth time here is 8.37am and the hominids are setting off for work. I've located a small area of greenery within New York, and of what they call 'A park.' It looks quite desolate here and has a green carpet on it, with flourishing shrubbery and tall things that branch out. Now descending. Yep, that's cool … I've landed.

Well, upon opening the dome, climbing out the saucer, activating my invisibility shield and setting foot on land, I'm met with a very strange smell indeed. I did argue, back home, that I would prefer not to have a nose and mouth upon designing my body (with my brain frothing in a glass bubble,) but they insisted I required these things for the purpose of my visit.

The Draconian Clan

Everything seemed okay when I was assembled back home, and the higher models have no orifices whatsoever, so they're the lucky ones.

But, they need to appreciate just what it is greeting my nostrils! There's a pungent whiff of something really nasty and, upon inspecting my left boot, I discover I've stepped in something brown and sticky. It's like a squashed log. Consulting the databanks on my personal computer, I discover I've stepped in 'Dog shit.'

That's just bloody fantastic! My very first step on Earth, soiled!

I find some water in a nearby feature and wash it off, carefully keeping my eyes peeled for any more logs that might be lurking underfoot. Dogs?

I swiftly look these up and discover they're yapping, shitting, snappy-little furballs which offer companionship for the humans.

I do not like the look of these and am confused as to why such untamed beasts should be so swiftly embraced by the trolls. But, there again, contemplating them, I can quite understand the union.

It's quite mild in the park. I'm now approaching a bench and there are two trolls seated upon it, both lolling about. This is the first time I've seen humans and I'm not wholly impressed. Their behaviour is very erratic. It is curious because, observing others in the distance, this disgusting duo are slurring their words and swaying to-and-fro; lifting brown-paper bags to their mouths and consuming something that I can smell even from here.

They're now talking:

"I need a slash. I'll take me bottle with me as you'll drink the lot with me back turned. Stay ere an keep our space. I'll go behind that there tree."

In the park

I watch this thing with hair on its face, attired in a shabby, torn, dark-brown suit, clumsily approaching a sapling.

Before reaching it, he stops just short of me and stares directly into my eyes. I am suddenly apprehensive and remain very still, assured that my invisibility cloak is operational. The green light on my wristwatch confirms this. However, he doesn't budge an inch.

Very carefully, I dislodge my sidearm in preparation for defence. It is a matter of principle that I cannot, under any circumstances, be seen in my true form. I have been given strict orders to nullify any troll that should gaze upon my alien features, as Galactic High Command fear word of mouth reaching Baltazar himself. I was informed that the trolls love gossip.

That is why I am a lone hunter, for want of the human definition; to appear as low-key as possible.

What's he looking at? Surely, he can't see me?

"Wat was that?" the dismal thing enquires. "I'm sure I saw something move over there."

"Yer drunk, yer dirty old tramp!" the other hollers. "Ave yer slash an shut yer bleeding great trap up."

They are British ruffians, evidently picking the US to soil, travel and to live out their intoxicated existence, amongst the brown logs and paper bags.

A haze? Does my camouflage leave residue, or some kind of displacement? I'll have to find a reflector and have a good look at myself when time permits. Nevertheless, the Guv did assure me I've got state-of-the-art technology. I'm now looking at the ship, or where I know it to be parked, and there's certainly no undesirable side effects visible.

The troll then concentrates on the tree and unzips his pants. He soaks the plantation with a dangling hose and, consulting my databank, I briskly discover that in relation to the bum which disposes solids, the hominids have another organ to adequately relieve liquids.

"Wat was that?"

We have no need for bums and hoses. We just make bodies to suit our needs and our nourishment is pure universal energy. I am growing tired of these underdog primates and am just about to move on when, quite by chance, the troll turns back to face me while replacing his hose. He's calling to the other vagabond.

"There's something bad a 'brewing, I swear it. I was born psychic and can sense the supernatural. There's a demon over there. A bloody demon!"

"Yer dirty old snotbag, you ain't got no psychic stuff in yer," the seated naïve scorns. "Yer just high on spirits. Anyhow, if yer a psychic, why ain't you a rich old toff like the rest of em?"

"There's something bad a 'brewing, I swear it!"

Psychic? I speedily consult the particulars and find, to my surprise, that this filthy mortal standing before me may actually detect my presence by way of extrasensory perception. It is a contested phenomenon, though mercifully not very widespread among the troll folk. Nevertheless, I now deem it necessary to take action.

The tree-leaking vagabond ignores his mate and briskly

begins to move towards me, albeit drunkenly. I swiftly survey the park and find that it's relatively vacant. Fortunate for me. I then aim my sidearm at the troll.

"Come ere yer crafty old devil," he slurs. "I see yer ... I see yer!"

I pull the trigger and feel a slight ricochet as the mechanism pumps out a fantastic blast that dissolves the tramp in milliseconds, paper bag and bottle included.

After a flash and a bang, he's gone, with no trace whatsoever. The one seated has evidently witnessed the assassination and immediately jumps up in astonishment. Before he can even holler, I polish him off too.

After a flash and a bang, he's gone!

Peace and quiet resume.

I am now moving towards an interesting part of this quaint

city. Ahead, and just beyond the park, there is a road. Just prior to that, many well-dressed and civilised looking trolls are bustling to-and-fro on a footpath.

There are two sexes here. Females and males. The females cook and clean and the males work in something called 'offices' and 'factories.'

There accents are different from those of the tramps and enforces my conclusion that this landmass, like the others, must support immigrants from all corners of the globe. The databank tells me that this USA is actually friends with many other islands throughout and that it has something called a President. This must be equivalent to our High Command. The President is the ruler, with these hominids subservient to him. Actually, I do believe that he is now a she.

The pedestrians have all got small black boxes pressed to an ear and are talking into them. I have evaluated that these gadgets are some type of communication device and that the trolls are very heavily dependent on them. I am near a female and, thankfully, no one appears psychic here. She has bright red stuff plastered on her lips and her hair stands up like one of their high-rise dwellings. She's all legs, bum and appears top-heavy. She's stopped just before me and is clearly excited about her day.

"Oh my, well … Nigel just bought me the greatest diamond ring you can ever imagine, Macey. Yes, that's right, a diamond ring! After breakfast and well, you know, he jumped out of bed and produced it, begging me to be the one!"

After breakfast and well, you know? I guess she cannot wear the 'VIRGIN' banner like their unfortunate tin-can thing I obliterated in space earlier.

"Oh, yes, he's also taking me out tonight. Where? Well I don't know Macey. He's real gorgeous and …"

I tire of this wasteful blabber and push on, noticing machines on the road up ahead. All are different in shape and style and I grasp the fact that the trolls cannot fly like myself, being reliant on primitive motors to turn wheels which carry boxes. Drivers steer these ridiculous things on hard concrete surfaces, and of which intersect the city. They exude smelly toxins that reach my nostrils and I again curse High Command for supplying me with them. Nonetheless, it is not as pungent as shit.

There is a dwelling just beyond the bustling street that interests me. Since I have been conditioned to read fluent English (the USA and Great Britannia sharing kindred blood,) I am able to research possible avenues regarding the 1947 scout and Baltazar. Books, of all things, may enlighten my passage. The building ahead reads: 'BOOKS FOR YOU.'

However, the road is clogged with the primitive machines and I can see no clearing visible. That's where another technological beauty of mine comes into effect and no, it's not the good old teleportation trick. We are still trying to perfect this with promising results. Regrettably, test subjects experimenting with this science back home have met with some grisly results; two of whom were turned into jelly, another exploding upon transfer. Nonetheless, the scientists are unperturbed and so the enterprise proceeds.

I am equipped with an anti-gravitational jetpack. I engage the contraption and steer myself quite neatly above the troll's heads. It is advisable that I employ this method as I do not wish to be run down by the honking, smelly vehicles. Although I have been assigned this body, it is not indestructible.

Now I'm on the other side of the street and have to dodge certain hominids as they impatiently head for work. No doubt, the women will clean the strange clothes they wear and prepare sustenance, with the men toiling in areas of employment in more effective matters.

The bookshop is huge. It has enormous transparent windows and a door that swings back and forth. I'll have to be very careful as I enter. I do not wish to surprise the old troll woman seated at a desk and within. Her grey hair and haggard face reveal complete misery. There is a huge sign on the door and it reads, 'BUY TWO AND GET A THIRD FREE.' I shall not require a purchase whatsoever.

An old male troll departs the store, carrying a brown paper bag, and there is a simple ringing sound. I grab my chance and swiftly enter the shop before the door swings back into place. The ground floor of this edifice is virtually empty, with the seated hag busy reading a paper.

UFOs. Factual incidents. That's what I'm looking for. I read the catalogue headers above the many bookcases until I come to one called, 'PARANORMAL.' This is at the rear of the shop. I turn back and notice the hag now dozing. Humans require this to reinvigorate their bodies, though I am certain I was educated on the fact they sleep when the moon rises.

I pluck a book off the shelf and read the title, 'MY LIFE WITH THE ALIENS.' Confused, I open the tome and swiftly digest its contents. This is utter fabrication! The author, a woman in her late fifties, believes she's been abducted by people resembling myself and that she's had numerous probes stuck up her arse.

Believe me, if we did that, she'd have a blistering posterior for years to come. Also, she was taken to the Moon and danced on it. This is ridiculous! How can the trolls swallow such garbage? She's also convinced she's a casual abductee and that the aliens have taken her eggs and produced hybrid children. Now, I must ask, why on Earth would a superior race of beings wish to conjure a lesser race by way of genetic manipulation? The answer is, they just wouldn't.

I select another and find the same old crap. A man who believes he was chosen by a race called 'The Arions.' The Arions appeared as golden-haired beauties, who whisked him off to Mars, where he walked upon the surface collecting rock samples. Unfortunately, these were confiscated by the aliens shortly before his return. Also, he was hypnotised by them to forget the incident. Conveniently, he recalls the capture, trip, samples and godly discussions, busting their superior mind-control tactics. Funny that!

Ah! Now, this book looks interesting. The third and of which I now select from the spinal information supplied recounts weird tales from the past concerning crashed disc retrievals. If my buddies actually arrived here, and if they had to make an emergency landing for one reason or another, this might lend a clue. However, I'm just concerned at the sheer volume of sightings these trolls have made of UFOs. Our race, that of 'The Greys,' make infrequent visits. I believe the 1947 scout was the last up until now.

Hmm! That's fake. That's fake … that's fake. Wait, 1947 – The Roswell Crash. Who is Roswell? I begin to read this part with avid interest and am quite excited that I might have something tangible to report and to focus on. There's an image of a man holding up a sheet of tin paper with the heading, 'CRASHED WEATHER BALLOON MISTAKEN FOR FLYING SAUCER.' Well, that might just be so, but the calendar date has wetted my curiosity to the point of pursuing this nugget of information.

Apparently, a windowless disc skidded within Mackintosh Brazen's ranch, prior to spinning out of control, and subsequently smashed into a hillock, killing all the crew. Presumably, it was hit by lightning and succumbed to a very unfortunate fate. Personally, I know the squad of the 1947 undertaking comprised of four members; Alpha, Daybreak, Twilight and Dusk. Dusk wasn't so bright, though he piloted the craft and was elected their chief, much to the chagrin of the lesser officers. His skills as a competent navigator came into question during his training but, because he was a favourite with High Command, got the job and so it stuck. Yes, even we have (using the troll definition of the word) browned-nosed upstarts. Dusk was aloof and cocky.

Though the facts are inconclusive, I feel this may be a

starting point for the first stage of my investigation. There is no reference of an aerial attack from another source, suspecting Baltazar and The Royal Star ship he swiped, and no mention of an assault by the primitives either; so I guess it'd be in Dusk's nature to lose concentration and to become negligent. If this was the ship, I bet he survived the ordeal, the puffed-up scallywag!

Roswell? Wright-Patterson Air Force Base, Dayton, Ohio? Since I am in New York, I shall have to obtain a map of the landmass and compute a course towards this military complex. However, will it still be there? And, if so, will it house any possible survivors? If Dusk endured the crash with minimum damage to himself and was captured by the hominids, he'd most certainly talk. He did nothing but blab, anyhow!

The others were far more reserved, observing the strict code of conduct in remaining silent, if apprehended by the enemy. Old blabbermouth would certainly divulge secrets to the trolls upon interrogation, if vowed assistance or luxurious fancies.

Before I search for the map section, my eyes catch another book concerning Reptilians. This greatly excites me, and I pluck it off the shelf.

'REPTILIAN ROGUES – THE HIDDEN AGENDA FROM DRACONIA.' Well, since these trolls can't even get a simple rocket up to the moon and back (and yes, the Moon landing of 1969 was a complete and utter hoax,) I find it hard to believe they have gleaned knowledge pertaining to the suggested constellation and its people. I flip through the pages and read the tome within a number of minutes. This humours me to the point of chuckling, and I am surprised by this emotional response. I check to make sure the old hag is still asleep, which she is, before pursuing the elegant illustrations, evidently fabricated by a troll called David Hassler. He's the artist and author of the book. Here's a passage:

'The reptilian creatures based within the Draconian system have been manipulating mankind for eons, along with being masters of deception. They have the ability, once arriving on Earth, to shape-shift, thus blending in with society, while contriving plans to subjugate the world. They do not eat people, though enjoy sacrifices, along with practicing the subtle but deadly art of Voodoo. This ancient magical exercise was handed to the Africans by them, when they seized the Babylonian city and overruled it with their own ways and customs, upon an extensive visit. In effect, Voodoo originated from the lizard's home world, and is used even today, albeit covertly.'

What a load of tosh! Who the hell is this troll to publish such shit? Jeez! He's not well-up with facts. I flip through the illustrations and am struck by one. Hmm – that does uncannily resemble Baltazar. Yes, the old croc might even take a shine to it, being that the author's got his face near-enough perfect, but no – it's embellished nonsense and I replace the thing.

There's another book based on the lizards and, after a brief perusal, I return it. This one assures the reader they are actually the Crowned Heads of State, along with running the monetary system on this planet. Baltazar is smart, but not that smart. Nope, I'll have to stick with my primary mission and try and glean any information I can about the original scout team, before pursuing further leads. Baltazar was good at hiding and that's about the only strategy he accomplished with gold stripes. If he's here, he's probably secreted within a preferred dank cave, or a water lagoon. He loved water, old Baltazar ... oh yes, you bet.

I move on to the map section and easily discover a plan of this landmass. New York is here and ... ah, there's Ohio. Well, the base shouldn't be too difficult to spot, considering they are usually set in the middle of a desert, or some other secluded part of land; with dozens of strictly attired trolls pacing it. Yes, I'll take this paper with me. Don't worry, everything I touch (and while my invisibility cloak is active) becomes obscure.

I tire of this stuffy old crap and decide to leave. I pass the old hag, now making very strange sounds through her nostrils as she rests, and approach the door. Now, here's a problem. How does it work? Wait, I recall the departing male troll pushing it, so I'll do the same. But what of the bell? Won't it wake the dozing crust? I decide to be quick about it and dart out, not wishing to look back. I then engage my jetpack and effortlessly glide above the increasingly busy street, right back to the park where I incinerated the dirty old vagabonds.

There's something real nice about flying and being so lofty above the troll's heads. I actually snigger as I gently and expertly approach the chair the wino's shared, recalling the garbled nonsense they uttered, before carefully examining the greenery for any signs of brown logs. Upon touchdown, I see a peculiar looking creature frolicking with a very small troll. The creature is disgusting! Jeez!

And I thought the trolls were ugly! It's got a long face and has four legs, which it uses to pace the shrubbery, and is sniffing at anything and everything. It's one of these infernal dogs! It's now arching its back and, what's this? It's manufacturing a lengthy brown log from its posterior. Even from here, and using my ultra-sensitive nostrils, I can smell the stench.

After evacuation, it turns about to face me. Now its snarling and barking and getting quite upset. Don't tell me this bloody thing's psychic too! I raise my weapon and incinerate the pesky horror. Instantly, it explodes in a puff of smoke, and the young troll is gasping and shrieking.

It's got a long face and has four legs!

Time to make a hasty departure, I think. I glide towards my ship, climb up the stepladder and then set about launching. My first contact with this primitive race will have to be reported to High Command. I am certain Zoltak Zan II will be pleased with my progress. This is just day one! Imagine his surprise at me having so swiftly used my superior deductions to ascertain the whereabouts of Dusk and his merry little band of Greys. I'll get promotion for this, you bet.

I engage the engine and begin to ascend. The ship is still camouflaged, though I'll find a nice little secluded spot, away from the great metropolis, to recharge. The paper map will require careful scrutiny before I prudently plot a course towards the Air Force Base that pertains to know of the saucer crash of 1947.

*   *   *

Well, I've been travelling high for about twenty minutes now and find a small forest west of the great city. I have no name for it yet, though, and when I land, I'll calculate my trajectory to better understand the exact location. The day is still pleasant and the transparent bubble set around me, just above the complex flight-systems of the ship, reveal a cloudless azure blanket that spans the horizon. I have already noticed distant vapour trails in the sky and ascertain these to belong to the troll's primitive air machines which they call 'Jets.' I have some basic knowledge of these things. Apparently, they are launched from the ground and use hydrogen to make themselves lighter than air. They are slow, very slow, and prone to explode, due to the dangerous gases the stupid trolls insist on using.

The forest is quite beautiful. There are, what I now know to be, tall trees everywhere, with adequate shrubbery to conceal my ship. My sensors detect no trolls within the area, and I gather they are busy in their city, cooking, cleaning and working.

Upon landing, I shall deactivate the invisibility shield so that it may have a chance to recharge. I want all systems to be sufficiently replenished upon visiting the troll's Air Force Base. I shall also wait until nightfall to accomplish this new assignment. Consulting my databanks, the primitives are susceptible to greater hindrance during the sleeping hours, as their optics are not accustomed to lunar radiance.

There's a sufficient clearing, surrounded by towering plant-things, and I lower the craft. Again, I drop the landing gear and make a smooth landing. I consult the computers and deactivate the cloaking device, along with shutting down the Plasma-Warp-Drive. All is well. Before I leave the craft to inspect the area (owing more to my own personal curiosity,) I shall contact High Command, to apprise him on the necessary details. I consult the relevant communication device and push the 'CALL' button.

I wait, and wait … and wait. Bloody hell, you'd think he'd give me priority, considering I'm a billion light years from home. What's he doing? Ordering a new flush piece of furniture, custom made by the slave-beings of Shatadan, or watching the latest episode of 'Gorgeous Greys?'

Finally, a large holographic projectile of the guv appears just before me and he's looking as smug as usual. His huge cranium, which denotes supreme intelligence and rank, is particularly shiny today and his huge black eyes, the latest additions from 'Had-Your-Eye-Full,' capture every spectrum of light you can possibly imagine. He's classy and aloof and surveys me with a degree of haughtiness. He projects his thoughts to me mentally.

"I see that you have landed on the primitive world, Taffy. Since I deem this communication to be very important, I trust you have not called to moan about the new ship we have supplied, or that you've got no leads at present. On that note, I must advise that you're not returning your sorry-little-arse to this sector until you've located the crew of 1947 and eliminated Baltazar."

He's not very happy today! I clear my mind and transmit my own thoughts, as clear as crystal, to his immeasurable brain.

"Supreme Ruler, I bother your illustrious head to inform you that I have a strong lead concerning the whereabouts of Dusk and his crew. I have made acquaintance with this primitive Earth globe and am now busy plotting a course to an Air Base that may house the missing saucer. Though the whereabouts of Baltazar is unclear at this time, I deem it most probable that an interaction with the 1947 mission may furnish more facts."

He shakes his head.

"It is clear to us that the crew are dead," he enlightens. "Your mission is to connect with Dusk's headband, when you find the artefact, and to merge with it. This, as filed in your report and if you bothered to read it, will visually show you what happened to the flight of 1947. If Baltazar is connected, you'll know about it. This will embellish leads."

He's really pissed off! Has someone pranged his brand-new saucer? Or, has his misses demanded another holiday? I cleverly curb these thoughts, to avert seeping them into his unceasing mind.

"I understand, Supreme Ruler."

"The reptilian royal family grow impatient for news, Taffy. If you are unsuccessful with the mission, there may be consequences."

Jeez! I've only been here for the first part of an Earth morning and the bloody lizards are already spitting venom!

"It shall be accomplished."

"Excellent," he responds, limply dismissing me with a hand. "And don't report back until you have positive news."

The image of him disappears and I'm just sitting there, in the ship, seething at His Worship's arrogance. It's alright for him, lounging in his gleaming palace, with hordes of servants administering to his every whim. The bloody butthead just snaps his fingers and it's all done. I should think that if he had an arse on that 1st Generation Body of his, they'd wipe that too … with silk linen.

I collect my thoughts and decide to venture outside, to get some fresh air. After all, it's got to be cleaner than that

New York City grime they inhale back east. I am furious that High Command supplied me with a mouth, having to inhale this shitty atmosphere and to talk in grunts, just like the trolls. Bloody butthead back home needs to stick one of these holes in his head and see what I mean. He'd soon come to appreciate just what it is us 3rd Generation Models have to contend with.

I climb down the exit hatch and reach the floor of the forest. Cautiously, I look around. No brown logs, thank goodness. I am not activating my personal camouflage at this time as it too, like the ship, is on recharge. I want everything to work at optimum efficiency when I visit the Air Base tonight and I have another little trick up my sleeve, so-to-speak, upon arrival. It's packed in the luggage compartment of the saucer and, after a little assembly, will be ready to do my bidding.

The air here is cleaner, and I draw it in. I hear strange sounds coming from the coppice and notice feathery things flitting about. Consulting the databanks, I discover that these creatures are called 'Birds.' Birds, as I come to understand it, flutter about all day and shit all over the place. Their primary function is unclear, though I suspect they add to the contamination of Earth.

My sidearm is at the ready, should I come across any unwelcomed visitors, and I set off down a small track, telepathically instructing the saucer to lock up. I don't want a troll getting in there, tampering with the sophisticated hardware. Though they'd never be able to pilot the ship, they might inadvertently blow themselves, and it, up.

Peace! Surprisingly, pure and blessed peace. It's even quieter than Noona, my home world. I require this time to compute my next venture and to try and conceive a plan in breaching the troll's security, in order to access the supposed underground facility of Wright-Patterson Air Force Base. I wager they have a little compound above, just to compliment the scenery; masking a warren beneath, and where they hide dark secrets.

I check the perimeter, just to make sure there are no unwelcomed visitors, and find a grey rock to sit on. I like to blend in with the scenery. I then pull out the paper map and scrutinise it. As far as I can tell, I am in a place called Allegheny National Park. Now, upon observing the chart, I need to travel south to Pennsylvania first and then on to Ohio, steadily steering in a westerly direction. It clearly illustrates the airbase on the map at this location. Very handy for terrorists. There's also someone called 'Burger King' marked in red, just short of the area. He must be a very important troll to warrant such a glittering inclusion.

Upon folding the map, my attention is swiftly drawn to something, or someone approaching! The sound is coming from a small footpath beyond and I steadily draw my sidearm from its holster. I do not, as of yet, engage my camouflage, as it's recharging quite nicely.

"I'm sure this is the way back to the car," a high-pitched voice matter-of-factly announces. "I marked the trees with yellow chalk and there's one of them over there. Look, you see it? On that tree."

Two middle-aged trolls, a female and male, appear on the track, both donning ridiculous hats and oversized sunglasses. Their clothes are utterly absurd. The woman troll has scarlet shorts and a bright-yellow sweater, with the man troll clad in a luminous-blue jumpsuit. He is puffing away on something propped in his mouth.

In the Forest

"Yeah, well … you're wrong!" he snaps. "We're too high up and, anyhow, other people mark trees with chalk. That's an old spot."

Where the hell did these hominids come from? I am unreservedly certain I had scanned the area quite thoroughly before landing. My astonishment swiftly turns to dread as I realise the saucer, now in plain view of the visitors, is not camouflaged!

"What the heck is that?" the man troll queries, raising a hand up to the ship. "It's a frigging flying saucer! Holy crap!"

"No it's not!" the female argues. "Don't be so daft. It's one of those new model homes they're promoting, that's all. Heck, they'll do pretty much anything to prize dollars out of folk. You don't seriously think one'll land right here and in the middle of the day, now ... do you? You need to go to Mexico to see that shit. You're so full of crap, Henry Betts ... so full of crap!"

I wait in absolute silence, cautiously observing the pair with my sidearm primed for use. Even though there appears to be debate over the origins of my vessel, the man troll proceeds towards it.

"And I'm telling you, dumb arse, that that there thing is a frigging flying saucer!" he excitedly exclaims. "We need to call the Ranger and have him come take a look at this Martian Mother."

"We're lost, Ball-Brains!" the woman troll hollers. "How the heck we gunna find the Ranger when we can't even find our frigging car. You're so full of shit, Henry Betts ... so full of shit!"

I begin to grow increasingly angry. This emotional response is erratic, though I am absolutely livid at the fact that my wall of privacy should so brazenly be interrupted by these bonehead rednecks. I attempt to weigh the odds against such an annoying intrusion – that I should be in the middle of a bloody forest and still seen – and it is this (and primarily this) which causes me to take drastic action.

But first, and before the stupid primitives are to be destroyed, I perform a quick and interesting experiment, just for the hell of it. I approach them and give them both a nod.

"Nice day, isn't it," I announce, waving my sidearm at them. "And, yeah – that there thing is a frigging flying-saucer. You're looking at a goddamn alien, though I'm not from Mars, you dumb arse boneheads."

The look on their contorted, ugly faces is priceless. They keel back in astonishment, the man troll dropping his smoky thing, with the woman cracking a fart.

"I'll just prize the nozzle of my extra-terrestrial sidearm right up yer nasty little butts and see how well you fare with a zillion volts pumped right up them."

I fire the weapon and watch as they both explode in a shower of sparks. There's a little piece of satisfaction in doing so, as my fury has reached boiling point. After the extermination, it takes a moment or two for me to actually simmer. This mounting aggression, I rationally calculate, must surely be something to do with exposure to humanity. Perhaps I am unwittingly digesting their native hostility. The air is, I feel, tainted with belligerence. Even so, it may serve to better aid my agenda.

On the face of it, it's probably not a bad thing, considering

Baltazar himself doesn't require contaminated air to make him the mother of all badasses.

Tuesday – 8th July 2027
Wright-Patterson Air Force Base

It's now 12.03 am Earth time and I have spent the duration within the coppice and near the saucer. She is now fully charged, along with my other necessary equipment, and I have mercifully encountered no other trolls throughout the evening and night. I have used the time wisely in perfecting my strategy and, after that, studying nature; namely the birds that flit and shit, tweet and twitter. They are, I have to admit, pleasant enough, though become annoying at times when quarrelling. I have noticed them eating the black and red bugs on the ground, and it dawns on me that this entire planet is quite literally one huge pecking order.

Big bad Wolves, I have ascertained through my personal library, like to eat little trolls in the woods, dressing up as hags and hiding in timber shacks, where they trick the youngsters into believing they're something called 'Grandma.' I have seen none of these in the wilderness, though suspect they are lurking about. The adult trolls are lucky, as there is no record of what feasts on them, other than things in the sea called 'Jaws,' should they happen to enter the ocean. Steven Spileburger made a documentary on this, which I have yet to watch with avid interest.

Noona, my home world, does not have any bugs, big bad wolves or Jaws. It contains only the supreme deity, moronic slaves and us, along with our fantastical technology, and is a haven for the elite. Baltazar's lot, back in the Draconian system, have millions of different primitive things hopping about their swamps and steam baths. That's if they survive! The greasy old lizards eat anything and everything, as they're not fussy. Hell, if the old Croc's arrived here, which we suspect, he'd even polish off the trolls as a main source of diet. The Draconians are big, really big, and stand upright; Baltazar himself reaching just over three meters. He's sort-of short for a dragon, with the royal family towering a staggering five meters.

Contemplation has been good. The birds have retired for the night, but the bugs do not seem to require rest. Upon observing them on the rock, they are still marching about, and appear as clueless to their surroundings. Earlier, when the birds landed to feast on them, they casually dodged the victims, as though it were just another day in paradise.

I walk back to the saucer, unlock it and then climb up the ladder. I seal the ship and, now seated within the dome, input the coordinates I have prudently calculated towards the troll's Air Force Base. The orbiting lunar sphere, now high above the forest, offers a cool luminosity and I can't help but admire this pleasant night.

I engage the engine and the ship begins to throb, smoothly rising as I steer it towards the star-spangled immensity of space. Wright-Patterson Air Force Base will be approached with caution and, upon nearing it, I shall engage my invisibility cloak. I am aware they have obscure tracking systems, though I can adequately fool these into believing there is nothing actually zipping about their airspace.

The journey is quite uneventful, as I have pre-set the course into my sophisticated navigational system. This does, at the very least, afford me an opportunity to observe the sleeping world from above. I shall reach my destination in around ten Earth minutes. I can travel faster if preferred, though it is unwise to engage lightspeed velocity within a planet's airspace.

Dipstick, a member of our very own 'Space Cadets,' made a stupid error by engaging lightspeed during a training exercise on a backward world and within his saucer, while manoeuvring across a mountainous range. The explosion was so terrific, the remains of him and his ship are actually etched in rock, where he crashed. There is a memorial plaque, in gold (yes, gold) beneath the engraved embarrassment and of which is a reminder of his idiocy. Never open the throttle so close to land.

The troll dwellings below are adequately illuminated by candles. A candle is a slow-burning torch made from earwax and sustains luminosity to better aid their deprived vision, while the planet turns away from its star.

From this vantage point, they do appear quaint. It is a very sleepy time for the primitives, as they must regain their strength for the new cycle; repetitively cooking, cleaning and working. The man troll labours for something called 'Money' and this thing is very important on Earth, especially for the Fat-Cats. These things drink cream all day and purr when they are loaded with the stuff, becoming stout as they indulge in the finer things of life. Fat-Cats govern the greenery and sometimes fire nuclear arsenal at other Fat-Cats, if they accumulate more wealth than what they personally hold.

I become bored of the scenery and decide to tune into one

of their news channels. My computers can translate portions of their signals to suit my own perusal. This news channel is a twenty-four-hour thing, as some of the trolls prefer to stay up and absorb the nonsensical drivel, while playing on their X-Fox machines. X-Fox are developed by a company called Microtoff and this system has a rival, the Play-Nation.

The holographic projection of the troll's news channel reveals a female dressed in a bright-yellow outfit. She wears a fixed, false grin and addresses something about the President. I listen keenly to the broadcast.

"Today, Madam President of the USA has addressed NASA officials in what seems to be a most bizarre mandate, pertaining to floating anomalies caught in the Earth's gravitational field. Most are reported to be meteorites."

Meteorites? The bloody planet is always bombarded with them, so what's new?

"It has been agreed that, as from this day, any foreign anomalies on approach will be destroyed by NASA's new and technologically advanced Disintegrator Gun; the most powerful weapon conjured to date and of which employs Quantum-Pulse-Destructors to accomplish its goal."

Does that include flying saucers?

"The President's recent breakthrough will help protect mankind from outside threats, regardless of their origins. Considering Professor Hawkman's warning, regarding a possible extra-terrestrial invasion and of malice intent, she feels it necessary to take action in globally shielding the world from external sources. She has always reiterated that the Voyager satellites, dispatched decades ago – carrying information regarding us and our position in the cosmos – were grave mistakes, which could wrongly be interpreted as an invitation to dinner. She calls this new protection 'A blessing for all.'"

Regardless of their origins? Shielding the world from external sources? An invitation to dinner?

They show an image of the President, undoubtedly addressing some troll conference or other, talking about their latest innovation. Although the humans are ugly, I suppose she would be what you'd call quite a stunner through their eyes.

"The Disintegrator Gun has raised concerns from other countries, with them suspecting ulterior motives from the President and NASA. However, Madam President assures them that there is nothing to fear. We can all sleep much better at night, knowing that this cosmic wonder is efficiently patrolling space, to defend all borders from peril; regardless of international grievances and political differences."

The newsreader smiles again and cheerfully announces that someone called Mr. Trumpet has taken quite a dislike to NASA's expensive 'Ray Gun,' and refers to it as a 'Universal Threat.' Mr. Trumpet is rallying for support in having the President removed from office, with him wishing to take the helm. I believe Trumpet had a turn, but was very unpopular. Undisclosed friends of his have warned that he actually wants to get his anxious little digits on the machine himself, to sort out Mexico. It would save the expense of a wall, in any case.

I shall have to investigate this Disintegrator Gun of theirs when my mission is done, and report back to High Command. I am just a little concerned that the trolls have not only advanced up the scientific ladder in such a short space of time, but also plan to zap anything and everything on approach to Earth. In hindsight, I was incredibly lucky! Disintegrator weapons of this kind have not, to my mind, been adequately realised by this semi-intelligent race. They can launch tin-cans into the stratosphere, bombard others with radiation bombs and even send simple electronic signals throughout the globe; but Quantum-Pulse-Destructors sounds suspiciously off-world to me. That kind of clout is distinctly used by the Draconians.

Could Baltazar be assisting the Americans? Does Madam President know him? This new information is disturbing!

There is a gentle chime from the ship, informing me we are close to the troll's Air Force Base. I engage the cloaking device and peek out the dome. Yep, there it is! Way down below, I can see a vast clipped area of land, with a number of illuminated flightpaths intersecting the station. Hangars, buildings, aircraft and vehicles encompass the region, and I select an uncluttered portion, swiftly descending. Upon dropping, I activate my 'Subterranean-Seeker' and unsurprisingly appreciate the fact that the crafty old scallywags certainly do have a vast underground complex.

My ship then detects portions of my own technology from within this warren and I briskly ascertain that it is, in actual fact, Dusk's very own headband. This is wonderful news! With it, I can gather facts and respond accordingly. The incredible nature of my discovery is only marred by the fact that the crew of 1947 are not, as far as the computers can tell, within the vicinity. No matter. First thing's first.

The ship gives a gentle bump as the landing gear hits the grass and I disengage the engine. I then sit there for a while, watching the base with my excellent vision. There are soldier trolls some way off, beside the huge meshwork enforcing the place, drolly moving about like automatons, stupid rifles slung over their shoulders. They appear as hapless and bored as a Draconian reading Baltazar's journal. Most are producing smoke from their mouths, flicking ash here and there, with others gabbling.

Considering my ship has blinded Wright-Patterson's detectors (that I am invisible to the naked eye,) I climb down to my luggage compartment. I don't require more arsenal for this mission, but I do necessitate assistance.

That's where Jax comes in. Jax, which High Command personally christened, is a mechanical minion. He does not take on the form of us, rather; he's fittingly constructed to handle great weight, along with accomplishing important or tiresome tasks. Basically, he's an automated slave.

Jax will create a diversion while I enter the base. He's also virtually indestructible, with the Earth weapons having little or no effect on him. I've just got to spend about twenty minutes assembling him outside. Yes, outside! When connected, he stands just under 4 meters, so there's no room within the saucer.

Jax is now ready for activation

He will be activated via telepathy when I am upon the entrance to the base. I have already prepared my infiltration plan and am assured that, while my gleaming buddy passes the time by distracting the enemy, I can slip within Wright-Patterson and seize Dusk's much needed headband.

If there's one thing I've learnt about military compounds, it's their insatiable desire to lie, if faced with infiltration. A complete obliteration of the site would be denounced by those of High Power, so my little adventure is sure to remain classified, once it's realised they haven't a bloody clue what happened.

I release a valve from within, and a large box drops from the undercarriage. I then exit the craft, collecting a few tools on the way, before opening it. Jax comes in three parts. Legs, torso and head. He's quite chunky for a humanoid servant and has a bluish tint about him.

High Command thought a splash of colour would do the world of good, considering the stereotyped silver much favoured by our people has virtually turned us colour-blind!

I spend the duration assembling him.

Jax is now ready for activation. He, like myself and the ship, has an invisibility cloak, and of which he'll use sporadically.

I then attach some braces to the underbelly of my craft, for his secure departure, which will – I'm certain – be swift. No part of our technology, not even a simple screw, can be left to the whim of these bozos. In any case, Jax is not expendable, with High Command reminding me that his creation was nothing short of an eyesore, considering the minerals used to perfect him. In human terms, he's what they'd call expensive.

With the robot standing beneath the saucer, momentarily camouflaged, I swiftly make my way towards the main entrance of the base which leads underground, and of which was shown on my schematic.

I whip out my sidearm and pass several guards without

incident. One of them is talking to the other.

"Jeez! I need a slash. You cover my back while I take a piss. I don't want the rookies spotting me. The slimy bastard's will report me to the General and he'll grease my arse!"

"You just unzip that big fat arsenal of yours and empty yer pool. Anyhow, the rookies can't see you here … they're way off."

I can feel the coolness of the air as I approach the hangar that greets me like a silvery upturned smile. It appears to be made of tin. How primitive. Below the arched structure, I see the entry point my holographic map revealed and of which leads to the trolls' secreted burrows. There are two sentries posted here, both appearing as jaded and lifeless as the others. I turn back to where the invisible saucer is and command Jax to clank over towards the first set of guards.

I watch with avid interest as he becomes obvious, fluidly moving his sophisticated joints. His squat head, protected by a translucent sphere, casts orange hues as his numerous indicators flash to life. He's humming a ridiculous rhyme! Where the hell did he get that from? Did he pick it up back home, when they were testing out his electronic neurological brainwaves?

"HUMANS, HUMANS OF THE EARTH, YOU FIGHT ALL DAY AND HAVE NO MIRTH. YOU MOAN AND GROAN, YOU WHINGE AND WHINE, AND FOREVER STATE YOU HAVE NO TIME. YOU PROTECT YOUR CASTLES, LANDS AND MOATS,

YOUR PRIMITIVE AIRSHIPS AND QUAINT LITTLE
BOATS. I AM THE TIDE THAT WILL WASH YOU
ASIDE, A FORCE TO BE RECKONED WITH AND
FROM WHICH YOU CAN'T HIDE."

I now know that it was Hooga, our chief scientist back
home, who was muttering all this crap when devising Jax's
brain, so the crafty mechanical minion has evidently
sucked his drivel up like a sponge to a stain. However, the
mood aptly compliments his motives, which are to
basically cause as much confusion and chaos as possible.

I observe the first two guards I encountered whirling
around, their faces dispelling uncertainty and horror.
The robot is now extending an arm and waving at them, a
troll custom. I actually have to give Hooga more credit
than he deserves in knowing something of these creature's
mannerisms.

"HELLO BOYS. WANT A GAME OF HIDE-AND-
SEEK? I BELIEVE IT'S QUITE POPULAR."

He vanishes for a second, having activated his invisibility
cloak, and reappears behind them.

"NOW YOU SEE ME ..."

He vanishes again.

"NOW YOU DON'T!"

An alarm sounds and it is quite clear Jax has been spotted
by the others. He grabs the soldier who took a slash and
briskly tosses him over his shoulder, before concentrating

on the other.

"HELLO BOYS!"

"Jesus!" someone exclaims. "What the hell is that?"

Jax now has hold of the other troll and bends him over a knee, smacking his arse as a mother would tan her son's sorry-little hide.

"SPANK THE TROLL, SPANK HIS BUM, SPANK HIM GOOD AND HARD. TOSS HIM TO THE DEMON TROLL, WITH LITTLE OR NO REGARD."

He then throws the man over the fence and sets his sights on the main bunker. The officers guarding the door swiftly pump a round of ammunition into him, with little or no effect. Other trolls hurriedly appear from within and I seize my chance, craftily slipping inside, with the pathetic humans contending with their new and ferocious foe.

"Call the General," someone commands above the din of bullets and cries. "He's gunna have a fit upon seeing this son-of-a-bitch!"

"CALL THE GENERAL, CALL HIM NOW ... ROLL HIS FAT RUMP OUT OF BED. LET HIM CAST HIS BEADY EYES, UPON THIS NEWFOUND DREAD"

It appears to me that Jax is developing a flair for poetry and would be better off attending The Royal Academy of Arts. Nonetheless, I am sufficiently satisfied that he will have the trolls busy for some time and, careful to dodge a barrage of anxious men now heading towards him carrying grenade launchers, I venture deeper into the complex, targeting the simple lift-thing which my schematic exposed, and of which will take me down to my destination.

I reach the lift and understand it requires a summons. There is a small button positioned to the side of it and of which I push. An unassuming indicator above the thing tells me it's currently on '–5' and, after a chime, it begins to rise. Jeez! It's so bloody noisy! It's also slow.

"The General's been alerted and has ordered a number of choppers to get airborne this minute," a panic-stricken soldier hollers, leading more troops towards the exit. "He'll monitor the assault from his room."

"What the hell is that?"

Yeah! That's about right! The grand-old General will park his enormous rump before a smattering of primitive television screens and observe the battle from within the comfort of his tin base, no doubt puffing on a smoky-thing the troll's favour.

BING! The lift opens. Surprisingly, it's empty. I would have thought there'd be more primitives piling out in an effort to combat my mechanical marvel. I enter the brightly lit box and observe a control panel. I select '–5' and wait for what seems like an eternity to reseal. Upon doing so, it begins to descend.

There's a mirror to the rear and I peer at it, content that, apart from the mundane doors behind me, it's vacant. I secretly admire our technology against these simple Earth dwellers and express no concern for the overhead camera; swivelling about in an effort to catch any unwanted recruits from reaching its hall of dirty secrets.

Finally, I reach my destination and the doors part, revealing a bleakly lit corridor. I step out and immediately notice that, further down one end (and where I need to go,) there is an electronic tripwire. I cannot fly over it, or crawl beneath, being that the bloody thing is positioned at inaccessible intervals, undoubtedly hooked to an alarm. There's also cameras attached to the ceiling. I blast them first, before concentrating on the main barrier. The explosion is quite violent, and I have to shield my eyes from it, turning from the volley of debris, smoke and flame.

As predicted, this triggers an alarm. Unperturbed, I glide down the corridor. So far, no trolls! I reach an intersection and recall, using my superior memory, which direction to take. Right. Upon taking this route, I discover another lengthy passageway and realise that this, too, is equipped with tripwires. Again, I utilise my weapon and destroy them, wisely pausing until the aftermath has cleared, before heading on towards a single metal door.

Now I can hear trolls approaching from behind, though they are some distance away. The ceiling above gives a violent lurch and there is a sudden audible 'Bang.' I see cracks forming in the roof and understand that Jax is effectively keeping the military busy. It is during this time that I suffer a feeling of both anticipation, euphoria and dread all rolled into one. Never in my existence have I ever experienced such an emotional burst quite like this. If this is a human sentiment and one of which is derived through drama, then I envy them.

The silver door ahead has a peculiar hand-print mechanism beside it. I check my back to make sure the coast is clear before firing. I do not release the trigger this time, preferring to run the cobalt beam across the alloy where it buckles, melts and dissolves. The door is now liquid goo on the floor. I glide through and discover, to my relief, that Dusk's metallic headband is sitting neatly within a small glass cabinet and upon a nifty little stand.

I smash the glass with the butt-end of my rifle, snatch the artefact out and thrust it into a small container attached to my armour.

"Someone's in the 'Alien Artefact Chamber,'" a male troll shouts from beyond the room. "The door's been melted. What could have done that?"

I turn to see a bald man, wearing a white coverall and strange-looking goggles perched on the end of his hideous nose, pointing ahead, with a group of armed soldiers amassing behind him. I gather he's a scientist, for his bland, absurd attire denotes a troll with no personality whatsoever. He is, I calculate, consumed only with a desire to understand and back engineer extra-terrestrial technology … namely that of my brothers. My anger swells to boiling point.

"Get your arses in there on the double and check it out," he snottily commands, aggressively waving them in. "The enemy may be able to induce invisibility … so be careful."

Unsurprisingly, he's certainly up with our gadgets and clearly suspects otherworldly intervention. I guess he's not astonished, considering he's hording my brother's tech.

I drift up towards the ceiling using my jetpack and comfortably pass the soldiers upon their advance. I then glide over the agitated scientist, lowering my weapon, and fry his sorry-little egghead to a complete and utter cinder. The army men are too preoccupied with their investigation to notice the demise of the uptight researcher. He slumps to the floor, virtually decapitated, while I progress towards the lift.

Once inside the primitive elevator, I acknowledge the control panel, pushing the designated button and wait. As the door cumbersomely slides forth, I feel another violent tremor throughout the complex and the lights momentarily flicker. I decide to remain hovering in the air, my insatiable desire to leave this dump growing stronger by the second.

'BING.' The elevator reaches the surface. As the door opens, I find a mass of trolls screaming, scrambling and fleeing back through the base. A searing cobalt beam of light pierces the interior and there is a massive explosion, the force of which knocks me back in mid-air. I slam into the mirror, cracking it, before briskly coming to my senses. I also hear gunfire and the sound of small rockets being fired from outside.

"He won't die!" someone shouts from deep within. I pop my head round the corner of the lift and peer through the exit, observing confusing blurs of Jax as he hurls a helicopter into the air, evidently having seized it in mid-flight. "We can't even scratch the bloody thing!"

"METAL DRAGONFLIES AND METAL BIRDS, YOU ARE PUNY TIN-PLATED DISASTERS. YOU FIRE YOUR PELLETS AND DROP YOUR CRACKERS, BUT YOU'LL REGRET HARASSING SPACE MASTERS!"

I decide to leave the complex and mentally communicate my position to Jax. I don't want him firing his weapon at me, or flattening me with a mangled metal dragonfly which he's become so fond of tossing. I exit the lift and head straight for the vacant doorway. There are troll bodies everywhere!

I make a break for the saucer, commanding Jax to permanently engage his invisibility cloak and follow. As I glide over the decimated carnage caused by my mechanical warrior, I am awestruck at the level of destruction he's caused. I see a number of crumpled aircrafts scattered about the land, along with other pieces of incomprehensible wreckage (flames hungrily licking away at them) and estimate that he's flattened half the aerodrome. I can hear troll gunfire in the distance, along with another metal dragonfly swiftly gliding overhead. This one is sweeping a powerful searchlight across the greenery, the pilots within desperately trying to locate the robot, and I notice several soldiers peeking out it through an open side door, pointing portable missile launchers down at the ground.

Jax is in hot pursuit as I swiftly approach the saucer. Though we are equipped with forcefield technology, I consider it a small mercy to have parked well out of range of the conflict. The less distraction I have, the better.

Now upon the ship, I command the robot to halt beside it as I gain entry, climbing up into the flight deck and preparing for take-off.

Inside the domed aperture, I observe the metal dragonfly in the distance, sweeping over the carnage and unquestionably befuddled by the swift disappearance of the mechanical man. A fresh battalion of soldiers emerge from another section of the aerodrome and I briefly discern their attentiveness as they nervously peer this way and that, rifles at the ready. A small explosion ruptures a section of it and the night sky briefly lights up, augmenting the devastation.

I privately consider the fallacy of these so-called secret bases, and of which denounce the collection of extra-terrestrial artefacts. Their efforts to back engineer my own people's technology is a sham, considering they're still utilising pathetic air-induced crap, which is not only noisy, but also extremely hazardous. If they had perfected such equipment, they'd have colonised their own moon years ago. I wager that Dusk's headband has eluded them to the point of disbelief. In any event, I am excited to learn just what it was that transpired during his flight back in 1947.

The saucer begins to hum, and I launch, prudently hovering over Jax. Aligning him with the fitted braces, I then activate their magnetic properties. I feel a slight jolt throughout as he is forcefully elevated by the mesmeric powers, clenched to the undercarriage like an Earth ragdoll; his limbs flailing about as we sweep up into the starry night.

The weight distributors of my ship kick in, compensating for his cumbersome load, and we set off, arcing across the heavens in a westerly direction. I decide to head for a remote region (and I mean remote,) whereby I can settle the ship on some mountainous province to conduct my analysis of Dusk's headband. I shall also contact High Command once I have sufficient information and when the next phase of my mission is organised.

Passing over sleepy fields, I suddenly feel a disconcerting lurch within the ship, and of which has taken the gravitational systems by surprise. A chime announces all is not well. The saucer declares that we have just shed half a ton of weight and I rack my brain for answers. It's only when I survey the readings once again that I find Jax missing. A swift sweep of the underbelly camera confirms he is not attached to his braces. I see a shadowy figure spinning and glinting in the moonlight far below, freefalling.

Within a few seconds, he disappears altogether.

I hit the brakes and then sweep down towards the area in question. Apart from the fields here, there is a smattering of dense trees. I am furious that, as chance should have it, he's crashed into them. It couldn't be within one of the troll's farmlands, where it's square and flat, nor within a clear hillock to enable swift intervention. No! Bloody trees!

I'm now forced to park on the perimeter of the grove. As I descend, I reduce speed and drop the landing gear. The region is quite dark, with the trees up ahead appearing formidable. When I cut the engine, the ensuing silence enhances a degree of trepidation and I cautiously peer around the dome to make certain I am alone.

I suddenly feel a disconcerting lurch within the ship!

I then use my sensors to scan the area before departing. No trolls in sight. As I leave my chair, I am satisfied that the camouflage technology is still operational. Collecting my sidearm, I then head straight for the lower deck, climbing down towards the exit hatch.

I am seething. Bloody robot! I am certain he was secured to his braces upon departure. I leave nothing to chance. I wonder if he were tampering with them during flight (getting ideas above station) and felt a-cut-above the ship, believing he could fly! Yes, that's it … he thought he could bloody well zip through the atmosphere like Super-Troll. I'll give him a grilling upon seeing him if, that is, he's not smashed into a zillion pieces.

I'm now out of the craft and inspect the magnetic braces. It's absolutely clear to me, upon examination, that he's prized himself off them. There are four slight indentations on the base of the hull, where he's forced his great bulk free. I shall, when he's reattached, deactivate him until required. The ship, like him, is not cheap and I'll probably get a rollicking from High Command for damaging Imperial property, once they check it back home. It'll fail an MOT under those conditions.

There is a strange animal honk coming from somewhere behind, and a bird flits over my head, momentarily startling me. There are more of them chirping in the trees and I wonder if these creatures actually sleep? I raise my sidearm and decide to float towards the grove, preferring levitation in this neck of the woods. I don't want to spend the duration washing shit off my footwear.

Apart from the odd sounds of nature, all is quiet. I cannot, as of yet, see Jax. The great lummox must be close, and I deem it safe to activate a searchlight built into my nippy armour to clarify his position. I enter the coppice and sweep the beam around. Nothing. I glide deeper and, after a moment, see him lying face down, within a small crater he's managed to form upon impact. He seems to be intact, with no outward signs of damage; though I'll have to try and stir him first before examining the hidden parts. I'd rather the big old brute move, save me having to lug his fat arse back to the saucer.

I telepathically command him to respond, but get nothing. I then approach his rear and flash my torch on his back. This is where his brain is stored, and I swiftly understand why he is not reacting. The panel covering his delicate neurological network is missing and, upon making a thorough examination, I discover that several components are absent. Fortunately, they're based on a sort-of 'Click-And-Connect' system, so I merely have to locate the modules and reinsert them.

But time is precious, and the bloody idiot has managed to plaster half his brain over the coppice. I am simply furious. I decide not to quibble about it and begin my task, methodically searching the grassland for the black chips. There's one! I scoop it up and realise that there's another fourteen to locate. Okay, so that was just beside him. I run my torch around his rear and find another two. I reinsert them and then carry on with the task. There's another and another and … what's this?

Six meters from Jax, I discover a shard of metal sticking out of the ground. It does not appear to be any part of him and the reason why I'm so attracted to it is because it's luminous. I approach it and decide to touch down, kneeling within the filthy soil. I prod the alloy and, after careful scrutiny, realise that it has a familiar quality. It also appears to be attached to something much larger, evidently buried within the earth due to me now tugging at it to try and prize it free. It simply won't budge.

I then decide to engage a nifty little device attached to my wrist and of which may be able to analyse the metallic components. I address the system, punch in its instructions and then wave it over the peculiar fin. A shaft of blue light engulfs the thing, and, after a number of seconds, it reads the compounds, breaking them down to form a picture of where the actual thing came from.

"THE COMPOUND DOES NOT ORIGINATE FROM EARTH," it cheerily announces. "ATOMIC CRYSTAL STRUCTURES DENOTE DRACONIAN TECHNOLOGY."

The declaration completely winds me and I back off, shocked and momentarily disorientated by the stark revelation the computer has made. Impossible! Surely? The sheer coincidence of me having zipped down from the heavens to retrieve a boneless robot, only to discover a spacecraft from the Draconian Empire buried in the bloody soil, is too much of a fluke. Collecting my wits, I advance towards the jutting fin and reanalyse the thing. Again, the computer is adamant that the material does not originate from Earth, but from the croc's home world. If it belonged to Baltazar, it'd be massive. Immense! I mean, as well as interstellar travel, the Royal Star ship was also built for comfort. It was even equipped with a miniature lagoon for the elite reptiles to wallow in, splashing and submerging till their heart's content. To dig it up would take weeks, maybe even months. Could he still be inside it? Did he die in its apparent crash? I need answers and I need them fast.

The first thing I need to do is concentrate on the robot. I don't intend expending a microbe of energy seeking a door or opening on the buried ship because the great lummox can do that for me. I'll have to conjure a makeshift shovel, or something to that effect, for him to use. Employing any form of Photon-Blaster may damage it and eradicate evidence. I can't afford to risk that. In any case, Jax is designed for labour. He won't strain a muscle, considering he hasn't any.

I return to him and set to work seeking the last of the missing chips. I could activate him with a number of them missing, but that might spell disaster. The absence of several logic-circuits (if you consider Jax to be logical) may cause him to become trigger happy, or downright assertive. He might even decide to pursue his dream of becoming Super-Troll and wreak havoc across the globe. In any case, I cannot leave a single trace of us behind. No, they've got to be here and within the coppice.

It takes me about an Earth hour to recover the lot, though I am spitting venom and cursing at the four winds for the postponement. One of the chips was nestled beneath his fat arse and another in a bird's nest. In a bloody nest! I hovered up to check the branches and found it there. The impact must have catapulted it right up into the twig-lined-case and, had it not been for my vigilance, I would have missed it entirely. The beaky critter occupying it tried to peck my nimble fingers, though a brisk swat cured the problem. The bird had been guarding oval-shaped turds, keeping them nice and warm under its smelly belly.
The peril of the robot, and the chance discovery of the Draconian Star ship, has considerably vexed me. I knew the mission was going to be hard, but this is ridiculous. If

the thing in the Earth did belong to Baltazar (and there are few, if none ever recorded venturing this far out into the galaxy,) then he's either in it, dead or long gone. The crash must have been astronomical due to the vessel having so effectively ploughed into the earth and I estimate that it would not have been a happy landing. Just like Dusk's! But what caused it? As far as the records show, which were supplied by the Draconian Royal Family, it was fully fuelled and in excellent condition just prior to being pilfered. A trip to Earth, even at the immense trajectory it took, would not have drained the tanks. Not even by half. Was he brought down by something? Or did the old croc lose concentration and smash it into the primitive world?

Pondering this, I have to thank Jax for his mindless behaviour. As a matter of fact, I estimate the chances of finding something on this scale to be higher than High Command honouring me a holiday. It's just fantastically ironic that we should stumble upon such a find and in the most arbitrary manner.

I reinsert the last of the robot's chips and, after checking things over, replace his covering. I then activate him using my own lingo and, low and behold, he flashes to life. He's still face down in the soil, but a number of flashing lights beneath his brain box raise my spirits. A low throbbing sound emanates from his thick casing. The sound intensifies as he reboots. The brute is back in the land of the living. His camouflage is currently down, and I have also lowered mine for the duration. I consider there being no point in expending energy while veiled in darkness and within such a solitary district.

"BODY ALL AKIMBO, FACE IN DIRT, I AM NEVERTHELESS FINE, NOT HINDERED OR HURT."

"Stop that nonsense and rise," I command, already pained at his ridiculous poetry. "You have work to do."

He rises and turns about to face me, his colossal bulk gleaming in the meagre moonlight. As far as I can tell, the titanic monstrosity appears to be unscathed. As a matter of fact, the only thing required of him is a decent clean.

"I require you to do some digging for me," I continue, pointing over towards the peculiar metal fin poking out the ground. "I shall have to fashion you a shovel. We cannot use Photon-Beams as they may destroy the ship."

"SHIP?" Jax asks. This utterly astonishes me as he's never actually asked a simple question before. He's also curbed his verse garbage for the duration. He turns to inspect the metal. "YOU CALL THAT A SHIP?"

"It's part of one," I inform. "The rest may be buried down below. You'll have to dig it out and find a doorway, or entrance of some kind."

"DO YOU HAVE A SCHEMATIC OF THE VESSEL? WOULDN'T IT BE PRUDENT OF YOU TO FIRST CHECK BEFORE DIGGING? IMAGINE THE TIME AND EFFORT THAT MAY SAVE US. IF THAT IS A TAILFIN, WE CAN ROUGHLY CALCULATE WHERE EXACTLY THE SHIP'S ENTRANCE IS BY WAY OF MEASUREMENT."

I am virtually speechless! He's not only become practical,

but also downright blunt. I'm also winded at the fact that his suggestion, however haughty, is exceedingly rational. My Goodness … they've given me a bloody Know-It-All! "I shall consult the ship's computer for a possible plan," I assure. "You stay here and don't move or touch a thing until I return. I shall fashion a makeshift shovel for you to use."

"SO, I DO ALL THE DIGGING?"

"How dare you question your superior officer's instructions!" I scold, glaring up at the brute. "You do not tire, so it shouldn't bother you. Just remember, you are my soldier and slave. I command you and you will obey me. Am I clear on that point?"

"INDEED. I AM YOUR SOLDIER AND SLAVE."

"Indeed."

"INDEED."

We momentarily lock eyes and I wonder if he's actually being sarcastic? I then regally glide back to the saucer, elevating myself so as to reinforce my position above the mechanical upstart, before thinking what best tool he can use to prize the soil free from the buried ship.

How dare he backchat me! As the ambience of the night surrounds me and I effortlessly reach the saucer, I consider Jax's impudence to be something quite disturbing.

If this is Artificial-Intelligence, then I'd happily bin it in favour of a mindless automaton.

He rises and turns about to face me

The days of old on our home planet were far happier and simpler when we utilised mind-numbing diggers, workers and the like. These new editions are, I feel, haughty and quite unnerving. It's the unpredictability of such things that justifies extra caution. I remind myself that he is nothing more than a fusion of metal and conductive elements. In effect, he's no smarter than a piece of space debris, or the passing of a cold, unpredictable comet.

I enter the saucer and climb up to the cockpit. There I sit, first checking on my aloof minion, before addressing the databanks. I command it to search for details pertaining to Draconian star ships and, a moment later, receive the files. I am supplied with a beautiful schematic of the vessel in question and of which I transfer onto our version of Perspex. Jax can have this, since he's smartly concluded how the overall operation is to be conducted and can bloody well get on with it. Indeed, and upon examining the diagram, I see that the craft does have a tailfin. An entrance hatch is positioned below it and at a peculiar angle. Unsurprisingly, the doorway is, like its creators, huge.

I have not, as of yet, had time to check on Dusk's headband, though that can wait for the duration. The more data I have to report back to High Command, the better. I'm sure the indolent, ancient old crony will almost fall off his throne when I furnish him with my developments. I shan't mention Jax's fall and how this ultimately came to reveal the hidden Draconian craft. No, I'll twist that little fact to my advantage. In any case, I'm sure the guv doubted my abilities and was perhaps even humoured at the thought of Baltazar having me for dinner. The croc is so formidable, few of my people, if any, openly volunteered for the assignment.

"Taffy will do it!" they all said as I recall the moment. "He's smart enough. Supply him with an appropriate body

and send him to Earth. He'll destroy the croc."
I exit the saucer and swiftly glide towards the coppice
where my haughty mechanical slave is waiting. He
appears to be chirping to himself and, when I reach him,
find a number of birds sitting on his shoulder, some
excitedly twittering and hopping about. It appears he's
joining in with the fun.

"I see you've made some friends," I sarcastically muse,
handing him the schematic. "A word of caution, they shit
on anything and everything."

Jax gently takes the diagram and examines it. He then
turns to face the tailfin and begins to clank towards it.

"I AM INFORMED THAT THE SHIP CRASHED HERE
IN THE SUMMER OF 1946 AND DURING A
BEAUTIFUL AFTERNOON," the robot announces.
"THOUGH MY NEWFOUND FRIENDS WERE NOT
PRESENT AT THE TIME, THIS KNOWLEDGE WAS
HANDED DOWN TO THEM THROUGH
GENERATIONS IN CHIRPS AND WHATNOT. THE
DAY OF THE CRASH WAS MOMENTOUS, AS THEIR
GREAT-GREAT-GREAT-GREAT-GREAT-GREAT
GRANDPARENTS WERE CELEBRATING THE
ANNUAL HUMAN HARVEST BY WAY OF
PILLAGING WHAT THEY COULD FROM THE OPEN
STALLS IN THE TOWN BEYOND."

"Bah!" I exclaim, somewhat perplexed. "Who told you all
that crap."

"THE BIRDS."

My face must be a picture because I stare at him in absolute disbelief.

"You're telling me that those feathery-things that shit day and night furnished you with all that drivel?"

"UPON TRANSLATION, YES," he continues, "THEY ALSO SAW THE PILOT ESCAPE ON FOOT. HE APPEARED TO BE SLIGHTLY INJURED AND WAS LIMPING. HE WAS CARRYING A KNAPSACK."

"A knapsack?"

"THEIR VOCABULARY IS EXTREMELY LIMITED, THOUGH I BELIEVE THEY ARE REFERRING TO SUPPLIES FROM THE SHIP. A BAG OR CASE OF SORTS, PERHAPS?"

"This is ridiculous!" I snort. "Knapsack indeed! I suppose he had a fishing rod too, along with a transistor radio?"

The robot turns his huge head around to face the birds squatting on his left shoulder. To my utter astonishment, there follows a frenzied reply.

"NO FISHING ROD AND NO TRANSISTOR RADIO," he affirms. "JUST THE KNAPSACK."

Now, here's a test, if ever there was one. Jax has absolutely no knowledge of the Draconian Empire whatsoever. Not yet, anyhow. I'll only divulge matters pertaining to the croc as we draw close to the kill.

Losing my patience with Jax

"And what, may I ask, did this pilot look like?"

Again, the robot addresses the birds and they cheerily comply.

"THE ONLY WAY THEY CAN DESCRIBE HIM IS AS A HUGE CROCODILE. ENORMOUS! HE WAS WALKING UPRIGHT AND HAD SHARP, RED

BEADY EYES. HE SEEMED TO LIKE HISSING A
LOT AS HE MOVED ACROSS THE FIELD AND WAS
EXTREMELY CAUTIOUS OF THE TOWNSFOLK.
THEY WOULD HAVE KILLED HIM WITH THEIR
PITCHFORKS HAD THEY SEEN HIM. HE WAS, THE
BIRDS EXPLAIN, MASSIVE."

There follows more chirping from Jax's feathery friends.

"HE MUST HAVE BEEN HUNGRY FROM HIS
VOYAGE BECAUSE THE ANCESTORS SAW HIM
CATCH A FOX. HIS ACTIONS WERE SO SWIFT, IT
SHOOK THEM TO THE VERY CORE AND HE ATE IT
WHOLE. TAIL AND ALL. HE CAUSED ALL THE
ANIMALS AND INSECTS THROUGHOUT THE LAND
TO HUSH UPON PASSING THAT DAY. EVEN THE
EARTHWORMS HID."

I am totally speechless! At first, I hover there in absolute
astonishment at the unbelievable turn of events. My
mechanical minion has briskly learnt the art of bird-talk
and, in return, they have been feeding him with apparent
factual events. That these pathetic, flittering, pesky little
critters are able to intelligently converse with sentient
beings is not only bewildering, but also disturbing. I have
underestimated them greatly. I wonder if they talk as
much to the trolls as they do to Jax? Could they spread
word of our visit? Are they able to transmit their findings
to other bird-tribes throughout the land, invariably
reaching the surviving tyrant of the craft?

So, old Baltazar is alive! If their testimony is indeed true,
then the greasy croc is here and, as I suspect, very much
hidden amongst the tribal race of hominids. Compared to

their brief lifespan, his is immeasurable. The databanks had informed me upon study that Baltazar is close to four thousand years old and that, for a Draconian, is equivalent to a sixty-year-old troll. And, the worst of it is, they become stronger and sharper with age. He's got plenty of puff in him yet.

I consider the ship and decide that it still requires an internal investigation. There might well be a clue hidden within it. Perhaps some plan left on a dashboard, or a recording of his thoughts while passing through the great barriers of outer space. Searching for scraps is a longshot, though I am determined to accomplish my mission as professionally as possible.

I produce an unimportant length of metal I collected from the ship and drop it to the ground. I then aim my weapon at it, engaging the Photon-Beam and melting one end into a flat broad-blade, before concentrating on the upper end to fashion an extra-large handle for Jax. When done, I leave it to cool and then point down at it.

"This is your tool," I inform him. "You will dig deep and hard until you come to the spaceship door. The precise position of it is printed on the schematic I have supplied."

The great lummox peers down at it for a moment and then turns his attention to the diagram.

"THE TASK WILL TAKE ME ROUGHLY TWO EARTH HOURS TO ACCOMPLISH. YOU MIGHT AS WELL FIND SOMETHING USEFUL TO DO WITH

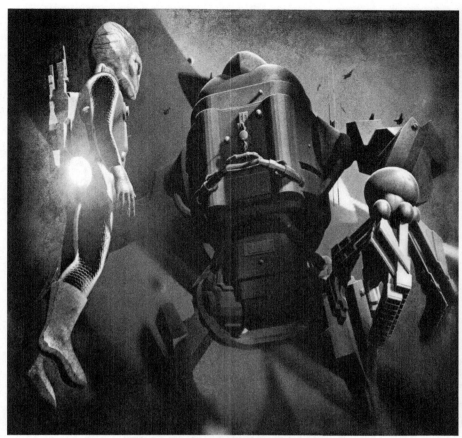

"Pick up the shovel and begin."

YOUR TIME WHILE I AM BUSY."

I am seething!

"You do not advise me on anything," I snap. "Pick up the shovel and begin."

He complies and approaches the tool, picking it up before giving me a good hard look. I am unable to interpret this temperament, but assume he is being downright aloof. When we get back home, I'll have Hooga take a look at his workings and ask that he makes considerable adjustments; namely downgrading Jax's personality chip. He's smug and snotty and I am finding this extremely challenging.

As the robot begins his task, the birds merrily flittering around him, I contemplate my next course of action; namely entry into the Draconian ship. Thinking about it, I decide that the great lummox himself can squeeze his fat arse within and peek about, rather than me. He's shorter than the crocs and sufficiently able to inspect the internal rooms, corridors and other reptilian whatnot. He's also equipped with a torch and can relay his findings to me live during the investigation.

To put it frankly, I don't relish climbing inside the thing. If I'm perfectly honest with myself, I'll admit that there's a degree of trepidation when it comes to Baltazar. To settle this miniscule dread and adequately lace it with a degree of logic, it is purely down to him being so utterly heartless. The complete lack of any sympathy, combined with a coldblooded soul, emanates through his glowing ruby eyes like the embers of a great fire. His appearance accentuates this dread and I actually quiver at the prospect of finally clapping eyes on him. Even his people are approached with a degree of caution when it comes to diplomacy, and it is rumoured that a number of otherworldly ambassadors were eaten upon stately visits.

Whether this was down to irritation, impatience or downright aggression on the Draconian's part, remains a mystery. Nonetheless, High Command's very own conference with them was conducted under strict measures. And I mean strict!

Upon the sanctioning of Baltazar's planned demise, the guv wore two layers of ionized armour, was encased in the toughest forcefield imaginable and equipped with a barrage of repellents, should the reptiles decide on having him for dinner. It went well and an agreement was made.

Basically, we kill the croc and they support us in the event of any future otherworldly antagonists plotting to sweep us aside. Personally, I'm not happy with the arrangement. If they can't eliminate Baltazar themselves, then how the hell can they prevent interstellar conflict?

I believe there's a far more sinister reason in taking the croc out of the equation. If so, High Command's not letting on. Not yet, anyhow. Could it be that they are able to smell one another's presence if assassins are dispatched? Are they telepathic, like us? I am befuddled as to an explanation and my mind is on overdrive as I swiftly turn to observe Jax busy shovelling dirt from the ship. He's making good progress. As a matter of fact, I am astonished as to how far he's actually reached; the tip of his head peeking above a mound of dirt. At this rate, he'll reach the door in no time at all.

I hover above and around him and begin to film his progress. This will be edited and sent to High Command upon my next report, along with the data I shall glean from Dusk's headband. I am certain he'll relay this promising news to the Draconian Royal Family, though unquestionably embellish the fact that it is he who is the ultimate crux of this entire operation, and not his minion.

"I AM NOW UPON THE HATCH," Jax announces. "IT IS SEALED."

"I thought you told me it'd take you around two hours to reach?" I sarcastically muse. "It's only been a matter of minutes."

"TWENTY-TWO AND A HALF, TO BE PRECISE. I ELONGATED THE STINT, JUST IN CASE I ENCOUNTERED A HICCUP."

"So, you're able to embellish facts," I annoyingly reflect. "Well, that's just great. I am supplied with a robot that not only backchats, but who also exaggerates."

"AND ONE THAT HAS SMARTLY DISCOVERED THE ORIGINS OF THIS CRAFT, ALONG WITH ITS PILOT."

"Be silent and open the hatch!" I snap, exasperated. "You can get your fat rump in there and sniff around for me. I shall monitor your progress from here. I require clues as to what the slimy croc was planning upon reaching Earth within the royal star ship."

"AS YOU COMMAND," Jax rasps. Again, I am left in limbo as to whether he's being sarcastic. Personally, I preferred his rhyming.

The entrance to the derelict ship is of typical Draconian design; a dull goldish metal, being segmented and giving the illusion of scales. The door itself is oblong and roughly four meters high, with a width of around two. The robot examines it carefully for a moment before rapping it with a hand. There is a disconcerting resonance and I actually take a moment to appreciate just how big the star ship is. This section alone is miniscule, compared to the magnitude of the buried vessel.

Jax then punches it and there is an almighty bang. The sound causes me to flinch, though I am delighted to see that the alloy has already bent inward considerably, prior to him pulling his huge arm back for another strike. Goodness! I wouldn't want to be on the receiving end of that! Bang! Bang! Bang!

He breaks through, feels around for something and then grasps it. Finally, the huge door begins to drop, and I understand it to be based on a simple gravity mechanism. As it descends, Jax activates a powerful torch attached to one of his shoulders.

"Excellent. Now, go inside and explore. Be extra vigilant, mind … it may be booby-trapped. At times, I shall direct you, should you happen to miss something important. I shall observe your progress from here."

I activate a forward holographic projection which is transmitted from Jax's optics and observe the appearance of a corridor within the cold vessel. The great lummox is not in the least troubled and briskly clambers within, the sound of his heavy feet thumping along the cold metal floor. His powerful torch adequately illuminates the area and, to my surprise, the outlook is excellent. Further down the bland walkway, there are two intersecting passages: stern and bow. Jax sagely decides to proceed towards the cockpit and, after a turn, disappears from my peripheral view.

"THIS SHIP LACKS ANY FORM OF COMFORT," I hear the robot groan. "I AM SURPRISED! YOU

WOULD THINK THAT THE ROYAL FAMILY
WOULD HAVE A CARPET IN HERE, OR – AT THE
VERY LEAST – SOME REGAL FURNISHINGS."

I ignore his grievances, keenly observing every facet of his
progress. Indeed, and privately, I agree with Jax; never
having actually entered one of these supposed luxurious
reptilian cruisers. It's as bland as High Command's
imagination and certainly lacks any form of cosiness.
Even our own ships, whether large or small, encompass
some degree of relief compared to this dull, metallic relic.
The unembellished golden hues of the walls reveal no
panels, etchings or logos. But, on the face of it, this
insipid environment sits well with the Draconian people,
for they are as gloomy as this dreary thing. Even the elite
are unconcerned with ornate baubles and pretty
furnishings, preferring their hot lagoons and endless need
for food; namely The Garborja; a rather large rat-like
rodent that breeds wild on their home planet and of which
is something of a delicacy to them.

I now see another door and it's ajar. Jax's enormous claws
come into view on the holographic projection and he
swiftly forces it back. Now we see something very
interesting as he glides his torch over the new room.

There is a skeleton of a Draconian lying rather untidily on
the floor. He, I assume (considering all centuries are
males) has a belt around the lower part and this, I
understand, held a sidearm. The holster is empty and,
upon closer examination, I see that the bones presiding
around the neck region are crushed. Baltazar must have
taken a bite to this sentry standing guard, prior to departure
and nabbed his gun.

"Jax, spin your beam across the walls," I command.

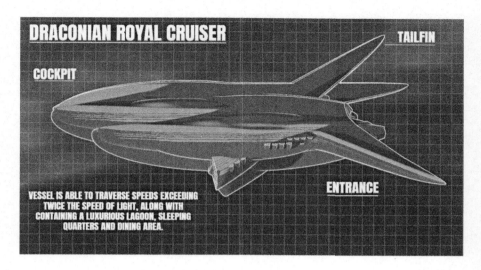

He duly complies. Yes! There's the evidence! There are dried bloodstains spattered across the metal and, as the robot drifts his torch ahead, I see it on the floor and leading to the next section of the ship. I experience a quick chill running up my spine from this disturbing revelation, before reminding myself that duty, above all else, matters.

There's another intersection ahead, though I concentrate on reaching the flight deck.

"Now proceed into the next room," I command. "This must surely be the cockpit."

He does not utter a word as he steps over the huge skeleton, advancing towards another door just past the junction. This one is different and, for the first time, has something written on it. It's a symbol and clearly denotes the royal family's crest; two serpents entwined in a planet … their planet.

Jax has developed an interest in it and runs his claws over the emblem.

"THE ROYAL FAMILY!" he booms. "THE EMPEROR AND EMPRESS OF DRACONIA."

"Yes, yes … I know all that!" I impatiently scold. "Can you open the door? That's what I need to know."

I watch him try, but there is nothing to offer grip.

"Smash it down," I command. The great lummox is good at that. "Prize it open like you did the entrance."

"WAIT … WHAT'S THAT?" he asks.

"What's what?"

"THAT?"

He is pointing towards an exceedingly small diode opposite the door, which is faintly, very faintly, flashing red. At first, I panic, believing it to be a crafty booby-trap … until the bloody robot goes and presses it. I flinch in anticipation of an explosion, or something dreadful occurring, until the only discernible sound is the weak purr of a motor.

When I finally have courage to examine the hologram, I notice that the door is sliding back.

"You absolute imbecile!" I rant, furious at his hasty action. "You could have blown us to smithereens. That could have been a trick switch. You fool of a fool!"

He lumbers through the opening without a word and his torch reveals, at last, the cockpit. My immediate shock is duly transformed to curiosity. The ship seems to have miraculously retained a degree of power and I hasten to feel optimistic at the mechanical man actually being able to derive some useful data from the retired computer systems. Jax is programmed to decipher Draconian linguistics.

There are four large chairs facing a dark screen. This, I assume, is their visual aid when flying. Just beyond the seating arrangement, a vast bank of computer terminals is sprawled out upon a golden dashboard. On observation, they appear lifeless.

"Now, don't go and smash anything up," I anxiously advise. "This is the very nerve centre of the ship ... the core of its records. Since you were able to activate the door, we may be lucky in finding a way to restore a degree of power to this reptilian rust bucket. Investigate a possible lead."

He moves forward, trundling towards the dashboard. There is an assortment of levers and buttons, along with other complex instruments adorning the console, and he nimbly uses one of his fat pincers to press, flick and explore.

"THERE ARE NO MORE ILLUMINATED DIODES IN HERE," he informs. "NOTHING SEEMS TO WORK, OTHER THAN THE DOOR."

"Just keep checking," I snap. "If there's power, there's hope. I do not fancy having to drift in myself to take a look, thank you very much. That's your job. I want every inch of that cockpit examined."

He moves to the left and takes a closer look at one of the consoles.

"THERE IS DRACONIAN WRITING HERE. NOW DECIPHERING LINGUISTICS."

He is stuttering as he slowly decodes the reptilian language.

"PO ... WE ...R!"

"You've just found the ignition button," I impatiently inform. "Push it and see what happens."

He moves a claw over the switch and presses it. To my immediate relief, the console screens sprawled out before the great lummox suddenly flash to life, and there is a distinct humming, emanating throughout the cockpit. A multitude of diodes begin to warmly glow on the dashboard as the system boots up. After a few seconds, the room glows a warm red.

I am now growing extremely confident of gaining some clues as to our reptilian monster's insidious plans. He, like most of his kind, are partial in keeping journals (just as we favour) and, being that he's militaristic, would fight the urge to resist a vocal log of his own affairs. One of the things about Baltazar is his efficiency with matters. He may be bloodthirsty, but he certainly isn't stupid. Anything but. Suffice to say, he's incredibly bright and technologically refined, able to whip things up that may benefit his goal.

The screens on the dashboard reveal statistics of the ship's current condition and it doesn't look good. One of them visually displays the power generator's status and it's virtually blinking on red. How this relic was able to stockpile the remaining surplus for so long is a miracle in itself.

"Quick, we haven't much time," I bark at the robot. "Instruct the computers, using Drakonian tongue, for any last reports made by the pilot. You're swifter at interpretation, being that your computerized."

Jax immediately responds, addressing the electronic brain of the ship.

"DU MEEKA, LAT-TAT, UN PILOTY DE CLAK UN VIRE-DE-LA-TAT."

There is a pause before the computer reacts. Its deep, monotonous voice is a combination of dialogue and hisses.

"SAR, FAR ... DE-TEE MAKKA DEL NAR TA-TA, UN-BARAGUNNA DE TAR, BAKKA MAT. BALTAZAR DU HIGH EN TRUT UN EARTH."

"What did it say?"

"THERE IS A SHORT JOURNAL, BASED ON HIS HIGH EMINENCE, BALTAZAR OF OLD," Jax reports. "IT'S NOW DOWNLOADING THE VOCAL TRANSCRIPT."

"High Eminence indeed!" I scorn. "Baltazar of Old should be Baltazar the Horrible. That's what we'll call him. What caused the crash?"

I wait, hardly believing our luck, and imagine High Command's face when I inform him that, not only have I found the abandoned royal star ship, but that I'm also privy to the crocodilian brute's continued existence.

The computer waffles on and Jax duly interprets.

"HIS HIGH EMINENCE, BALTAZAR OF OLD, WAS FORCED TO CRASH-LAND HERE WHILE ON HIS WAY TO THE OUTER RIM OF THE GALAXY IN ORDER TO ELUDE POSSIBLE CAPTURE. UNFORTUNATELY, HE ENCOUNTERED A METEORITE STORM AND WAS HIT, DAMAGING THE MAIN DRIVE OF THIS VESSEL, PRIOR TO PLUMMETING TO EARTH."

The robot then adds.

"IT'S NOW GOING TO PLAY BALTAZAR'S ENTRY."

I am recording everything and leave nothing to chance. So, the rascal was met with an interstellar accident due to, what I can only assume to be, either loss of concentration or computer error. Whatever the cause, he arrived on this dismal, backward lump of rock and is conceivably very much at large. And now we're going to hear his actual voice, this viper of the stars.

When the computer relays his entry, I'm struck by the rasping, deep, hissing monotones of Baltazar's voice. It is laced with a degree of authority; such is the haughtiness of this swaggering war criminal. Jax fittingly translates the audio message.

"SHIT! THE MAIN DRIVE'S GONE. BLOODY ROYAL STAR SHIP! IT CAN'T EVEN DEFLECT A SIMPLE METEORITE STORM; LET ALONE OUTMANOEUVRE THE RASCALS PURSUING ME. I'M HEADING FOR THIS CRUSTY BALL THEY CALL EARTH. IN ANY CASE, THIS UNFORTUNATE INCIDENT MAY WELL BE A SMALL BLESSING IN DISGUISE."

The robot pauses as he listens to the next entry before interpretation.

"THEY'RE CALLING OFF THE HUNT, PERHAPS BELIEVING I'VE PERISHED IN THE COLLISION, BUT I'M ACTUALLY NOSEDIVING TO EARTH."

I hear, on the recording, the sound of an electronic chime as the croc continues to waffle above the drone of buggered engines.

"YES, THE PURSUERS ARE DEFINITELY DEPARTING. WELL SOAK MY RUMP IN MUD, THEY'RE SCOOTING! GOOD RIDDANCE!"

He's now clearly agitated as he's hissing a lot.

"BUT I'M HEADING FOR THE BIGGEST BANG IN HISTORY! ALL GUIDANCE SYSTEMS ARE TOTALLY FRIED. I'M LICKED! I'LL HAVE TO TRY AND STEER THIS HUNK OF JUNK INTO THE

ATMOSPHERE, BEFORE ATTEMPTING A CRASH-
LANDING OF SORTS. HERE GOES … HERE GOES!"

The recording abruptly ends there, with no other entry. All
is dead and I command Jax to disengage power to the
crippled ship. He can rebury the exposed outer skin so that
the trolls don't discover it by chance and become curious.
I certainly don't want Baltazar to get suspicious, should
word leak out about the discovery of his buggered vessel.
Jax lumbers back to the exit. When he appears, I wave a
commanding hand at him and point back at the makeshift
shovel.

"Cover the ship back up and pack it good and hard. The
birds can shit all over it if they so wish, but I want it
looking like a hillock. We shall then proceed back to the
ship where I shall study Dusk's headband."

Jax picks the tool back up and immediately complies.

"I'M NOW BEGINNING TO GET THE PICTURE," he
rasps. "THIS SNAKE YOU'RE SEEKING IS WANTED
FOR SOME KIND OF TREACHERY BY HIS OWN
PEOPLE AND ACCIDENTALLY CRASHED HERE ON
EARTH, WHILE EVADING PURSUIT.
UNFORTUNATELY, THE RECORDING HAS NOT
ENLIGHTENED YOU AS TO A POSSIBLE LOCATION
OR STRATEGY. THIS DRACONIAN WAR
CRIMINAL COULD BE ANYWHERE. IF YOU ARE
TO FIND HIM AND KILL HIM, AS I SUSPECT, THEN
YOU'VE CERTAINLY GOT YOUR WORK CUT OUT
FOR YOU."

I am enraged at his cockiness and don't hold back.

"The matter is well in hand and I do not need your input, thank you very much. You just carry on pounding the dirt on that thing and chirping to the birds while I make an assessment of the data. In other words, keep your trap shut! You are useful to me only in matters of physical labour. Leave the brainpower to me, do you hear?"

I hover away from him, back towards the saucer, as I consider the new information. Upon reflection, I am utterly amazed that this place of bird-shit, trees and dirt is the origins of Baltazar's appearance on Earth. The royal cruiser was wrecked beyond all hope of repair and so, on that note, the croc trundled through these pastures on foot, armed only with a knapsack and pistol, to evidently seek refuge until he engaged his cunning mind to seek an agenda of sorts. But that was then. Back in 1946. Is he still in the US, or colluding somewhere else?

I am troubled by something that niggles at the back of my mind and it's to do with the American President. She made a universal announcement to her troll folk, informing them of a new weapon and of which can deflect any interstellar bombardment. Though the concept is to be applauded, considering these primates are as thick as two short planks, I am puzzled as to how this feat was attained. I will have to pursue this conundrum as I suspect Baltazar behind it. My train of thought then considers the fact of him having possibly evaluated my arrival, or interstellar advent, and so is taking vigilant measures.

Jax seems happy smacking the dirt hard back up on the ship and I decide to leave him to it. I re-enter the saucer and produce Dusk's headband. It's time to see what caused the Roswell Crash back in 1947, and why Dusk's very own mission in seeking Baltazar went so horribly wrong.

I place it over the crown of my head and close my eyes, connecting with the internal and ethereal memories it stores. I immediately see the crew of the old saucer. Since Dusk was wearing it at the time, I am ostensibly him in this present state. The ship, as stated earlier, has no portholes, and the three other members strapped within their quaint chairs are having a bloody argument! Typical. The view is slightly blurred, due to the tremendous speed they're travelling. Dusk is in command of the vessel.

"And I'm telling you to slow down!" one of the crew members barks at him from across their circular cockpit, shuddering in his seat. "We've already passed the stratosphere of Earth. Engage the breaks immediately. My own instruments tell me we're heading towards a desert of some sort and that a storm is brewing. The computers are picking up heavy electrostatic waves created by this and we must be extra vigilant. If we should crash into the breakers, it may disrupt the drive of our ship."

Dusk is extremely arrogant!

"Don't you tell me how to bloody well fly. I was created long before you and have a First-Class Record in aviation. Shit doesn't happen with me. The Leader himself decorated me for being the first clone to fly through a blackhole and successfully appear at the other end. That, I might like to add, also involved electromagnetic waves far greater than those of this puny little globe. Okay, so it took me fifty years to head back home, but I did it all the same. Just hold onto your artificial butts. We'll be landing presently, anyhow."

I see Dusk, from his perspective, peering down at his own controls and fumbling with the speedometer. He's bloody well increasing it!

"I'm afraid Alpha is correct!" the second crew member argues. "If you don't decelerate now, we may very well be heading for disaster. Also, the ship is travelling too low. We're skittering above land too close for comfort and so, on that note, I am going to personally lock you out of flight mode and take command myself. Are you boys in agreement with that?"

The others all nod.

"You got it, Daybreak!" they concur.

This fuels Dusk's arrogance beyond all measure, and I watch his fingers, with lightening precision, dart over the looming controls. There follows a pleasant chime and he now becomes rather smug.

"Well, you're too late. I've just disengaged your own authority over my ship. You'll find that your input will receive no responses. I am your Commanding Officer and you'll do well to obey and respect my decisions, based purely on stealth. The faster we go, the less likely it is we'll be tracked by the primitive radar systems employed by these bickering Human creatures."

"You always were a bloody joyrider. Cheap thrills and dangerous manoeuvres are your forte," Twilight snaps. "We have been sent on a very special mission and must respect the integrity of the ship. If we locate the Baltazar lizard, we will be decorated beyond all measure. In order to do that, we must tread carefully. You are abusing our agenda and playing with fire. This incident shall be reported to the Leader. Slow down this instant!"

There follows a huge and ear-splitting bang! Due to me wearing the headband and experiencing everything Dusk senses, the jolt takes me by surprise. It is clear they've hit something, for I feel a great crash and rise; the GeForces so terrific, my stomach lurches as I experience the spin of the saucer upon impact. I can see fleeting glimpses of dirt rising in the central hologram. An explosion tears a section of the ship apart. One of the crew members is whipped through it so fast, he's a complete blur. He cartwheels out the enormous crack, vaporized by the blast. It's Twilight! I guess there'll be no more backchat from him.

I hear a not-so-pleasing ring announcing trouble, with the saucer totally out of control. With the central hologram now buggered, I sense it slam into something humungous; the impact sending Dusk and others flying into the forward compartment, prior to being ricocheted back. An explosion, followed by a blast of light, blinds my view until, that is, all is still. I look around and find the crew dead, apart from Dusk. He is evidently crawling out the craft on all fours, escaping a small fire now choking the innards. Through the huge crack, I can see the twinkle of stars and, beyond them, the receding storm he flew them straight through.

Dusk then pulls the dead members out, one by one, before slumping down on land; eyeballing the huge hill he's managed to impale.

The saucer is trashed, and he lies there for a time, stunned and regretting his imperialistic manner above a concerned crew. He must have passed out after that because, the next thing I see is broad daylight. Upon waking, I discover an assortment of military trolls surrounding him, and he's quite dazed by it all. He tries to tell them where he's from

I guess there'll be no more backchat from him!

and that he's seeking Baltazar, but they simply can't understand a word.

"It was an accident, you understand?" he's telling them,

getting to his feet. "Although we can't repay for the damage caused to your squashed hill, we can certainly work together in making things all better. How about it?"

One of the trolls, bearing martial insignia and cradling a rifle, makes a comment to one of his comrades.

"Well, if that ain't county news! Last year, we had a report of a ship coming down with a bloody lizard limping to god knows where? Now, we have these marshmallow fellas with their spanking new ship all banged up. They need flying lessons from General Ramsbottom. He'd teach them a thing or two in these gizmos. Were they on Premier Lager or sniffing Elmer's Glue? Let's just face it, they can't steer the bloody things. We'll take this ship for ourselves and see what we can glean from it."

I am speechless! He's mentioned the croc! So, they knew about him having arrived, though through the pitiful titbits I can't glean much else. It is clear to me that they didn't find him, rather; knew of his existence through word of mouth. Perhaps the birds told them.

I then see the but-end of the rifle slam into Dusk's face and then its light's out for him. The headband reveals nothing more.

I remove the artefact and decide to contact The Supreme Ruler. I'm sure he'll find this new information to be of great value. I plug in and wait for a response. Nothing! I hail him again and, after a time, he finally answers.

"Taffy, I hope for your sake you've found Baltazar. I have just received a communication from the Draconian

Empire, demanding an update.

The saucer is trashed!

Their impatience continues to grow. I've managed to stall them, knowing fully that you'll only communicate with promising news."

"Indeed, Supreme Ruler," I nod. "Not only have I located Dusk's headband and gleaned the unfortunate demise of him and his crew, but I've also managed to trace the croc's ship. What's left of it, anyway."

"Excellent. So, where is he?"

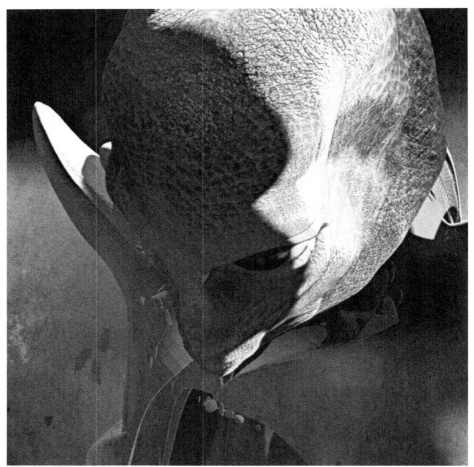

Supreme Ruler

"I'm still working on that. The crew you dispatched to Earth in the year of 1947 were killed by Dusk's arrogance, and nothing more. He decided speed was paramount and that was ultimately their undoing. He managed to smash the saucer into a hillock and was consequently captured. The human trolls mentioned a reptile having crashed prior to him, though the particulars are vague."

He's not very happy and I can read it in those very large

eyes of his.

"Well, you have three Earth days to find and execute him," he blatantly announces. "I've some very bad news for you, and no amount of persuasion can alter it. The Draconian Royal Family have ordered a new, state-of-the-art Planet Decimator into action. The signature of the rebel lizard, Baltazar, has evidently been detected by them, though they are entrusting you to polish him off.

The reason why they don't send their own bounty hunters is because he'll be able to smell them. You, my dear clone, are safe in that department. Due to his elusive nature, the Draconians fear a contrived assault, or some form of nasty repercussion. Consequently, they have instilled these measures to ensure the safety of their people. If you fail in your mission, the Earth will be reduced to a cinder when the weapon arrives in the Earth's solar system. It's currently en route."

I am quite speechless. Don't get me wrong, I really couldn't give a hoot about this race of pitiful creatures that swarm like ants across the planet's surface, but I feel pangs of guilt at the very thought of this globe being reduced to dust. Bloody hell! How impatient are the Draconians! Couldn't they just give me a little more time? Now the bloody fate of Earth resides in my hands.

"Can't they extend it to a week?" I query. "Three days is too short."

"No, Taffy … No! You must locate, film and destroy the brute before the weapon arrives. That's it."

He mulls something over in that vast cranium of his and appears slightly sympathetic now. Perhaps he too feels a twinge of responsibility resonating throughout that over-inflated ego of his.

"Listen, I don't like it any more than you do, but we have our orders. Contrary to popular belief, I do actually have a soft spot for the Humans, as they may just amount to something."

Was this emotional blackmail? Was he mimicking feelings, just to appear as a glimmering idol in the eyes of the reptilian elite? As far as I know, the lizards possess none.

"Just as the Draconians themselves crawled out of their lagoons during their evolutionary stage, and we hopped about as insects, pillaging the greens, Humans are progressing towards technological advancement. Yes, they're having a few tantrums and tiaras at the moment, but when the dust settles, we may see another superior race of creatures proudly rise to take their place among the stars."

He then becomes downright assertive.

"Just find Baltazar and kill him. Three days, Taffy … three days!"

He cuts the communication and I am left feeling rather perplexed. The weight of responsibility lays so heavy on my shoulders, I'm actually disturbed by an emotion of dread. What if I fail? What if the Planet Decimator arrives and fries Earth to a cinder? I'd have to scarper prior to extermination and evade home like the plague. I begin to evaluate the other lifeforms present throughout the cosmos and am depressed to find they won't accept refugees; especially the likes of me. The Greys aren't very popular among the stars, no thanks to some of my older brothers who turned rogue and started sticking probes up arses.

I shall have to get to work right away. My sense of anxiety transforms me into an impatient animal, and I head back out the ship, drifting over towards a cheery Jax who has completed his mission and who is now busy twittering with the birds.

"Get your oversized butt over here this instant!" I demand. "We are leaving for the capital of Washington. I am anxious to study The President of this land."

He turns to face me and gives a nod.

"AS YOU COMMAND."

I study him for a moment and realise he appears rather subdued about leaving his feathery friends. I can't afford to express compassion at this time as the fate of Earth now hangs heavy on my shoulders. The great lumbering mechanical lummox will have to say his goodbyes and return to the saucer at once, as every minute is precious. I'll fill him in with the particulars later, but for now, we must be on our way.

I hear a few pathetic sniffles coming from him as he lumbers towards the ship, with one of his little fellows shitting on his shoulder. Perhaps it's their way of wishing him well; either that or christening him 'Good Luck.' I pay no attention to it as I command him to shut down, prior to lift-off. I don't want a repeat of the last and embarrassing incident. I'll reactivate him when we reach Washington.

Inside the saucer, I call up the map of this primitive land and locate Washington. Something called The White House is where this stunner of a President troll lingers, so I compute the coordinates and then ascend; grasping Jax in the grip of the magnetic braces and ensuring our camouflage is faultless. With all systems running smoothly, and the ship announcing all is well, I sit comfortably back in my chair and watch as the little nook we visited disappears altogether, along with the Draconian Royal Star ship and disturbing memories of Baltazar.

Wednesday – 9th July 2027
Washington D.C.

Considering the muck and bird shit we experienced back at the nook, I am amazed as to how pristine and orderly Washington actually is. In comparison to the places I've already visited, this is like a quaint little Toyland, with its clean roads, stark white and silver buildings and immaculate lawns; all trimmed and pleasing from the vantage of the air. I whip over a park and see child-trolls merrily playing on peculiar looking structures, some spinning on a saucer-shaped thing with others kicking an orb about. I see a number of disgusting furry dog-things the human's favour and picture plenty of logs in the park. I catch one of these appalling creatures in their usual posture; back arched. After evacuation, the little snapper is sliding its arse across the grass, hindlegs up in the air, with its master giving it a grilling for seemingly showing him up before a group of female trolls.

Again, I pride myself on the fact of being pure in every sense. I cannot abide these filthy creatures, yet my heart tells me they do not deserve mass extinction by command of the Draconian Royal Family. I'm annoyed that this sentiment has evolved from the drastic measures imposed by them and I try to shake them off as best I can. I wonder if the Earth air is somehow contaminating me, reshaping my thoughts and opinions in favour of this childlike race.

I must concentrate on my task and feel no emotion. Yes, that's it! I must expunge sentiments and just get on with the job. This thought annoys me even further because, apart from myself, my bloody worker is already helplessly plunged into cheeriness with the natives of this planet. Where the hell did he adopt such annoying traits? He's part of an incredible race of clones, the very best in the cosmos, and he stamps about kissing nature and all that crap. I'll give him a dressing down when we're done here and make him see the wider picture. He'll learn a thing or two from me then, that I can promise.

The computers announce that we are making our final approach to The White House. With the invisibility cloak working its usual magic, we slip beneath the veil of the Supreme Commander's dwelling without incident. No troll-like tracking system can detect us, and I am resolute in keeping everything under wraps this time. Totally! The ship, myself and Jax will remain invisible as we carefully scout the pristine white building which is now coming into view.

The lawns are so extensive, I have a pick of where to actually land the saucer and I'm very pleased to see that it is well guarded. The fencing of this establishment is such that the common trolls are not permitted within and, judging from the stiff little guards wearing their ridiculous outfits (lining the dwelling,) I anticipate no trouble whatsoever. They are as lifeless as dolls, these servants of the woman troll who runs America. I have no idea if she's home or abroad, though I am greatly thrilled to be able to sniff about the house and to see where exactly it is she acquired the Disintegrator Gun.

NASA couldn't have built it, that's for sure. They're too busy tinkering with tin-can equipment and forging faked images of their space trolls landing on the Moon and Mars, to be smart enough to contrive such fantastical technologies. No, this is the work of Baltazar – that I am certain.

"WHERE EXACTLY ARE WE?"

With great swiftness, I pull the saucer over towards a batch of trees and glide it over them, gently dropping so that it's nestled nice and tight within. I then retract Jax and watch as his lifeless body makes contact with the ground; the titanic lummox slumping slightly as he comes to rest on terra firma. I disengage the engine and collect my pistol and whatnot. I then run a schematic snoop of the building but, surprisingly, find it appears to be jammed. This enforces my suspicion of an alliance with Baltazar.

I'll have to make it known to Jax that secrecy, above all else, is what matters here. He's not to make one bloody whoop of a sound … not even a whisper.

I depart the ship and hover over towards the robot, activating him. He shudders, twisting his head this way and that, evaluating his surroundings.

"WHERE EXACTLY ARE WE?" he demands.

"Keep your voice down," I curse. We are far from the patrolling guards, but I must emphasize some points here before we begin 'Operation Break-in.' "We are now in Washington and at The White House. The White House is where the troll's governor presides. We are going to investigate the building ever so quietly and without incident. Is that clear? I want to know where exactly it is she acquired the technology for The Disintegrator Gun. I suspect Baltazar behind it."

To my immediate annoyance, a number of birds swiftly flit down from the trees and align themselves on his shoulders, all chittering and shitting as he greets them with similar tweets.

I aim my pistol at them and vaporise the whole sodding lot. The blast is so swift, it takes Jax by complete surprise.

"THEY WERE JUST ABOUT TO TELL ME THE BEST WAY IN," he gruffly informs. "NOW, THE OTHERS ARE HESITANT AND WILL NOT COOPERATE!"

"Cooperate indeed!" I scoff. "We haven't time to listen to a bunch of pecking parasites, thank you very much and, besides, we've got one hell of a problem looming. A very big problem indeed. Pay attention to what I'm about to disclose."

He stoops over me in anticipation. I'm pleased to actually see him focused.

"Our Glorious and Supreme Leader has informed me that the Draconian's patience has now worn rather thin. Fearing Baltazar's presence here on Earth, the Royal Family have commissioned a new death ray upon it. It will arrive within three days and, if we fail to corner and kill the slimy bloody toerag, it's goodnight for all. They fear that Baltazar's up to something sinister and so, for peace of mind, intend to solve all their problems in one swift bang, along with your flittering, shitting feathery little friends. Three days, Jax. Three days!"

The robot thoughtfully stands to attention and contemplates the dilemma with considerable care. I watch him very carefully as he digests the facts.

"DOES THAT INCLUDE US AS WELL?"

"You, most certainly!" I heartlessly snap. "If we don't get that slippery croc, I'll leave you here to perish in the blast. You can share a tweet or two with your friends prior to obliteration."

He is completely unfazed by this and then responds with an impertinent view.

"AND HOW CAN YOU RETURN HOME WITH FAILURE WRITTEN ALL OVER YOUR FACE? YOU CAN'T, THAT'S WHAT!"

He laughs and my patience, like the Draconians, wears thin.

"YOU COULDN'T EVEN ESCAPE TO THE OUTER RIM, LET ALONE COSY US WITH THE REPTILES UPON SUCH A HUMILIATING FIASCO. YOU AND I ARE JOINED AT THE HIP, MR … AND DON'T YOU FORGET IT. I AM, I MIGHT LIKE TO ADD, RATHER EXPENSIVE, LIKE YOUR SHIP. IMAGINE OUR GLORIOUS LEADER'S REACTION IN LEARNING THAT YOU ABSCONDED ME, IN FAVOUR OF SAVING YOUR OWN ARSE."

"How very dare you!"

"ALSO, I WILL EDUCATE YOU ON A SIMPLE FACT OF MY OWN. OUR GOV INTENDS TO HAVE ME USED AS AN EDUCATIONAL TOOL FOR ALL THE NEW LITTLE DARLINGS HE PLANS TO CLONE WHEN THIS MISSION IS CONCLUDED. I, HE TELLS ME, WILL BE MOST BENEFICIAL IN CULTIVATING THE VALUES OF INTERACTION, TO NAME BUT A FEW OF MY ASTOUNDING TALENTS. IN SHORT, YOU'RE GOING TO HAVE TO PROTECT MY BUTT, AS I'M SURELY DESIGNED TO PROTECT YOURS."

Now I'm sure he's developed the art of lying. In fact, I'm certain of it. Him, being useful to the new cadets on Alpha Sector 3. Bloody hell! I actually laugh and this rather annoys him.

"I SUGGEST, IN LIGHT OF THE GRAVE SITUATION WE HAVE BEEN PROPELLED, WE BEST GET A MOVE ON. WE'VE GOT A CROC TO KILL."

I am exasperated with his sarcasm and merely nod.

"Not a sound, do you hear. Not a mechanical twitter, jingle, fart or whisper!"

I glide over the grass with Jax tailing. Mercifully, the birds have refrained from flitting about and I intently listen to the robot's footsteps. The turf muffles his weighty pace, though I can hear the faint sounds of his working innards. They're not too distressing, and I make a note of us merely keeping a distance from the trolls once inside the building. The Georgian styled mansion now looms ahead. I think we've landed at the back end of it, as the structure is tastefully arched in the centre. A jet of water is being pumped into the air, just short of it, and I wonder what function this entails? Perhaps the feature is used to quench the thirst of visiting trolls?

We spot two guards standing as lifeless as statues beside imposing doors and this is when I order the robot to halt. I immediately stop before the fountain and Jax does the same, turning his head this way and that and looking rather pathetic.

"WHAT'S WRONG?"

"If it hasn't already escaped that vast academic brain of yours, one of which our illustrious leader favours so much, we need to think of a way in," I whisper, turning to face him. "I'm not at liberty to use my weaponry here as any attention on our behalf would be disastrous. I am ascertaining a plan of action. Give me a moment."

He nods and places a huge claw on his domed mouthpiece, as though imitating deep thought.

"I HAVE A SUGGESTION."

"Really?"

"YES."

"What is it?"

"WE CLIMB UP ONTO THE ROOF AND SEE IF THEY HAVE A HATCH OR SOMETHING TO ENTER."

"I don't need to climb. Anyhow, how will you manage to grip the masonry? You might slip and cause a scene."

"I AM CAMOUFLAGED, LIKE THE SHIP AND YOURSELF, SO ANY RUCKUS CONCEIVABLY HEARD, SHOULD I LOSE MY GRIP, MAY RAISE AN EYEBROW OR TWO, BUT OF WHICH WILL CONSEQUENTLY GO UNNOTICED. I AM AN EXCELLENT CLIMBER."

Excellent climber indeed! I snigger at his marvellous delusions. Privately, I see the value of his idea, but will not dare congratulate it.

"Then let us approach the side of the dwelling and proceed with your plan."

He seems extremely pleased with my approval and punches the air in a pathetic sign of human victory. I cringe and make a note of having his creator back home reprimanded for infusing troll-like traits and of which are utterly wretched. He points to the left of the dwelling.

"THERE ARE NO GUARDS OVER THERE, SO I CAN START MY ASCENT."

He prudently leads the way and I follow, comfortably gliding behind him. I note that the turf has been neatly trimmed and I can detect no logs. Even so, I prefer to levitate above land. An old piece of turd might have already been discreetly compressed by a straying guard or gardener, and I wonder if Madam President actually has a furry pet thing of her own?

As we approach the left side of The White House, I am rather disturbed to see no footholds whatsoever for Jax to take. None. The masonry is smooth and dauntingly high. The area here is clear of humans and I can hear a bird or two twitter in the distance, within some trees just beyond. I hope, for their sakes, they stay well back, as we perform this daring feat, and I produce my nippy little ray gun, just in case the pesky little peckers decide to hop on my robot and start a conversation with him.

We're right up against the house and Jax is dithering.

"Well?" I sneer. "Let's see you get your fat rump up there, Mr Bloody Jim Bond."

"WHO IS JIM BOND?"

"He's a troll who defeats the baddies. Unlike you, I thoroughly researched this planet."

"THEN WHY DIDN'T OUR SUPREME LEADER ASK HIM TO DO THE JOB, INSTEAD OF MAKING US TRAVEL ZILLIONS OF LIGHT-YEARS TO DEAL

WITH THAT WRETCHED CROC?"

"If that were so, you'd never have made the acquaintance of your wonderful, flitting, feathery friends, now ... would you?"

"JIM BOND? WHAT DOES HE BOND?"

"I don't know. Anyhow, hadn't you better concentrate on the task in hand?"

Jax raises his head and observes the roof. It's quite high. He touches the brickwork with one of his huge claws and ascertains whether it's good for grip. It's not. The great lummox then takes a few steps back, jumping up at the wall with such force, a crack materialises right before our very eyes. He rebounds, expertly preventing a tumble, before embarrassingly brushing himself down and appearing rather coy. After that, all is quiet, except for the birds twittering in the trees. I observe him in mild contemplation.

"Climb the building indeed! You fool of a fool! You can't scale it with ego."

I reach for my gadget pouch strapped around my waist and produce a small pistol. It is not my nifty ray-gun, but a device that can fire a length of indestructible wire up to the very top, with a clasp at the end to ensure firm grip. I aim it up at the roof and expertly fire the thing, the clasp virtually soundless as it gains a foothold. I then tug at it and am pleased to note it is secure.

I hand it to Jax and point up at the roof.

"YOU CAN BEGIN YOUR ASCENT."

He tests the wire for himself and is satisfied.

"YOU HAVE TOOLS, I DO NOT," he rebuffs. "THAT IS NOT FAIR."

"That's because you're my tool!" I snap, jabbing a digit up at the building. "Now get your fat arse up there this instant."

I am surprised how efficiently he accomplishes this feat, though only due to my assistance. If anything, he's quite a good climber. I use my jetpack and glide upwards, passing him on the way. I give him a little wave, fluently reaching the top and waiting for him. He's still sore about my stylish equipment.

"WHY CAN'T YOU SUPPLY ME WITH A JETPACK?"

He's now clambering over the lip of the roof, his joints twisting as he skilfully clears the wall.

"Because you are not authorized to have one," I simply state. "Now, forget the natty Jim Bond paraphernalia I have at my disposal and retract the wire. We must keep this operation beyond top secret and leave no trace of our presence."

I turn to observe the roof. The windows here are too narrow for Jax to enter and so, with him trailing behind, we move along the south side of the promenade, towards a central-arched section which mercifully is double-doored, and of which allows entry into the dwelling itself.

Undoubtably, everything will be riddled with alarms, and so I produce a scanner, running it along the doors; safely disarming and unlocking the simple troll mechanisms.

I open the doors and wave Jax in. He must stoop very low to enter. There is a corridor and mercifully it is huge, allowing my robot ample room in which to manoeuvre, though his head barely misses the ceiling when upright. In fact, as I close and lock the doors behind us, I discover that The White House is gigantic. Peering down a lengthy corridor, I can see a central hall. This must lead to stairs. The Oval Office, I previously ascertained on the ship and after studying a map on the troll's internet, is set somewhere on ground level, though the particulars are vague. We'll just have to sneak around and find what we can. After all, how can anything go wrong? We're advanced and invisible and these stupid trolls will not suspect a thing.

Thankfully, nobody appears to be about.

We head down the passageway and I am not interested in the adjacent rooms, merely concentrating on reaching the lower level for documentation and records pertaining to The Disintegrator Gun and Baltazar's possible hand in the matter. If we can discover this, then it may give a clear indication as to where exactly the croc is hiding.

We reach the central hall and, to our immediate right, I see a staircase. There is also an elevator, though Jax is far too big for this, so we concentrate on reaching the easier and preferred route. The robot studies the stairs and turns to face me.

"WHAT ARE THOSE?" he whispers.

It suddenly dawns on me that he's never seen or used stairs before in his short and miserable life.

"They are what the trolls use to get about," I inform. "They are called steps."

He tests them with a foot, holding onto the banister. He almost slips and recoils in alarm.

"I MAY END UP IN A HEAP DOWN THERE IF I ATTEMPT THOSE STEEP AND STUPID THINGS."

I become extremely agitated and shake my head in frustration.

"Then what do you suggest? I carry you? You're such a nincompoop. Look, let me show you how it's done."

I gently drop to the floor and briefly disengage my jetpack. I then walk down the stairs, turning to face him before rising back to where he's looming.

"You see, it's as simple as that. One step forward, the other foot follows. One step forward, the other foot follows. Even a Chimpanzee eating a banana and clowning about can do it. Now, follow my lead."

He is hesitant, though actually accomplishes this with relative ease. But he is slow. Painfully so. I must contain my impatience as we reach the second floor because, at that very moment, two male trolls suddenly appear from a room, passing close by. Their neat attires suggest they've just rolled off ironing-boards. I virtually hold my breath and Jax sensibly stiffens, infusing me with enough confidence in accomplishing this little undertaking with little or no fuss at all.

"Oh, yes," one of them matter-of-factly announces upon passing. "Edward went missing last Tuesday. That's the thirteenth member of staff to disappear within The White House this year! I'm telling you, I'm handing in my notice, asap. The President can eat shit if she doesn't like it … I'm done-and-dusted here."

"I don't believe he just vanished like that, and in here, of all places," the other troll argues. "It's all horseshit! The President won't appreciate your resignation, that's for sure. She'll make you pay for it. You'll end up working at Wartmart, if you step out of line."

"Thanks a bunch!"

They both disappear into an adjacent room.

I wonder just what their mutterings meant? Disappearances? In here … The White House? I swiftly ascertain that the President is not as nice as first thought, considering she makes people work at Wartmart, if things don't swing her way.

"WE ARE STILL SKY-HIGH," Jax informs, breaking my thoughts and peering out one of the windows. "IF THIS OVALTINE OFFICE IS ON THE GROUND FLOOR, WE NEED TO BE LOWER."

"I know that!" I hiss. "And it's Oval Office, not

Ovaltine."

We approach the next stairwell and descend without incident, until we reach the ground floor. Here, the entire situation has changed, as there are many trolls milling about. Mercifully, the corridor is so huge, we can move against the wall unnoticed. I must state at this point that our camouflage even repels shadows, as light from the forward-facing windows illuminate the already artificially lit room. Due to our technology able to refract light particles, they are diffused the moment they bounce off us and so, to that end, we are virtually unnoticeable. I say 'virtually' because, depending on the natural source of the Sun and what angle it takes, the camouflage can sometimes suffer disruption; the incident with the Tramps back at the park clearly demonstrating this point. However, we are safe in here.

It's also hot down here. Unnaturally so! I am by no means efficiently acquainted with the humans, though skilled enough to understand their preference with tolerable comforts. This is unusual. The aircon's must be faulty, as the trolls are sweating profusely. I happen to approach a control panel, with one of these conditioning units merrily buzzing away, and discover the gage set at a blistering 45 degrees! There's another one, further down the corridor and, upon approaching it, realise it set the same.

Evidently, the President likes to bask in heat.

Personally, I prefer a cool 15 degrees, and Jax is the envy of cool, as he runs on -50. In contrast to these troll's technological clout, they went the other way in terms of conductivity. I must smile in having studied the pathetic history of this race, and of the recorded cases of fires caused by faulty wiring, or electronics, due to their insatiable obsession with heat. Even their microprocessors require fans to cool down, while calculating the crap they reel out, and this exasperating path can only worsen.

But hey, the boss said there's some promise with this race, so who am I to question the ethics of their industrial might?

I reactivate my jetpack, feeling more comfortable airborne, with the robot gingerly following. He is quiet for the moment.

Now, which door to take? I am annoyed that the schematics of this grand edifice are vague, though remind myself that I have enormous advantages over the inhabitants, along with possessing enough firepower to amicably blast my way out, should things turn drastically sour.

I halt for a minute and Jax does the same. He gently taps me on the shoulder and leans into me, whispering:

"THERE'S SOMETHING UNDERNEATH US."

I am confused and flash him a quizzical look.

"What are you talking about?"

He points to the floor.

"I CAN FEEL A VIBRATION COMING FROM

BELOW."

"Are you sure?"

"WELL, LET'S JUST PUT IT THIS WAY: YOU'RE
FANCIFULLY FLOATING ABOUT WITH YOUR
NIPPY ANTIGRAVITATIONAL DEVICE, WHEREAS I
HAVE MY FEET FIRMLY PLANTED ON TERRA
FIRMA. DOES THAT OFFER A LITTLE GLIMPSE
INTO MY LOGIC?"

He has a point, though I scowl at him for being so aloof.

"You're saying there's something to it?"

"INDEED. THIS PRIMITIVE DWELLING SEEMS TO
HAVE A SUBTERRANEAN LEVEL AND, UNLESS
IT'S OFFICIAL, IS EVIDENTLY USED TO SECRETE
SOMETHING UNWORTHY OF TROLL'S EYES."

"Well, I'm aware of that!" I indignantly scold. "I would
have discovered it myself, anyhow."

He stares at me for a moment and nods his head.

"INDEED!"

There's that sarcastic spice again! Jax then surprisingly
jiggles about like an enthusiastic toddler, clapping his
hands together.

"I'M BEGINNING TO FANCY ADVENTURES. IT'S
LIKE A SCOOBY-DOO MYSTERY!"

"Scooby Doo?"

"YES. I'VE WATCHED A FEW EPISODES WHILE
ASLEEP, TUNING IN TO THE TROLL'S
TERRESTRIAL CHANNELS, AND LOVE IT. I'LL BE
SCOOBY … AND YOU SHAGGY!"

He actually giggles and I feel a rush of humiliation
envelope me. I have no idea what he's babbling on about,
but am alarmed at him accessing Earth transmissions
without my approval. I want to clout him, but think better
of it in this delicate scenario we're in.

I'm annoyed at his childish traits, but rather puzzled as to
how he can become Albert Einstein in one sense, and a
tattling little snot in the other. He certainly is developing
an alarming multicomplex personality and I don't like it.
It makes him unpredictable and I hate fickleness with a
passion.

There is a door ahead of us which is slightly ajar. I glide
towards it and peek in.

"Look here," I say, turning to face the robot. "I think this
must be The Oval Office."

There are no trolls inside it, and I glide through, opening
the door wide enough for Jax to enter. I then quietly close
it after him, before inspecting our surroundings.

Indeed, it is oval in shape, with an imposing window at the
rear; a huge desk set just before it. Two cosy sofas face
one another mid-centre, with patriotic flags adorning the
room. It is neat, in any case.

I glide over to the desk for inspection. There is a primitive telecommunication thing sitting on it, with a number of papers sprawled about; several ink scribers sitting neatly in a holder. I am surprised to note there are no microprocessors in here, and circle the desk to examine the drawers.

The robot moves over to several bookshelves and starts to inspect the tomes on them. Since he is applying discretion, I leave him to it as I try one of the draws. It has a key in it, but of which is locked. The key is gold and elaborate, though I am befuddled as to why it is sitting neatly in the lock. How stupid is that! I gingerly turn it and slide the drawer open. Inside, a green book is visible. I pluck it out and open it up.

It's an exercise book of some sort and appears to be about torture. I am utterly dumbfounded at the contents of this thing, as it shows illustrations of trolls being roasted over rotary spits and in different positions. Other diagrams offer alternative methods of execution, and I wonder if the President secretly deals with rebels in this fashion.

The pictures have been professionally drawn and I must congratulate the artist for his perfect renderings.

"WHAT'S THIS?" Jax suddenly booms, concentrating on something within one of the shelves. "IT'S BEHIND THIS BOOK HERE. THE BOOK IS CALLED 'FANCY THAT!' IT LOOKS LIKE A SWITCH."

I am briskly surprised by the interruption and urgently turn to face him.

"Don't touch anything…!"

It's too late! The lumbering lummox has, surprise, surprise, touched whatever it is he shouldn't, and I steel myself for an alarm to sound, or for some hidden horror to briskly reveal itself in the form of security. I know we're camouflaged, employing state-of-the-art technology to confound the humans, but the thought of The White House discovering it's been infiltrated would not bode well with our agenda.

"You brainless, arrogant, annoying little …!"

There is a noise, but not in the form of a siren, or the swift gathering of guards for that matter. A pleasant electronic jingle sounds and the bookcase, where Jax is standing, swiftly glides open.

I stay perfectly still for what seems like ages, as the robot scrutinises the opening. My cloned heart is pounding so hard, I can feel my entire body shuddering. It takes me a good few minutes to recover from Jax's reckless action and I am seething with anger.

"The next time you do something like that, without my approval, I'll have you deactivated … permanently. Is that clear? Permanently!"

He is not listening; rather, studying the aperture.

"THESE STEPS ARE STRANGE!"

Assured this switch only opened a secret door, I glide over to the robot and peer in. It is dark in there, but the Oval

Office offers enough light to discern the foreground of a sinister looking stairway, leading to goodness knows where? I turn to face Jax.

"The subterranean level, I gather?"

"FANCY THAT!"

The steps are unusually shaped in as much as being wider than conventional ones. They spiral down and the ceiling is very high.

I turn to face the robot.

"You hold the door open, just in case it should shut after me, while I search for an inward switch. I feel it sensible we cover everything before exploration."

"INDEED."

I hover inside, activating my nippy torch and, to my relief, find an internal button. I then return to the robot.

"Now, after you," I smile, waving a hand inside. "And, be quiet about it."

"THANKS."

"You're doing me a great service."

"RIGHT!"

"Just get your sorry arse in there!"

I have no qualms in him activating his torch as he lumbers within, for any obscured assailant would only see the flare and nothing else. Upon detection, Jax would simply extinguish it, leaving the troll befuddled and shaken for a moment, to accept it as an unspecified anomaly.

I glide in after him and, not surprisingly, the door closes behind us. Apart from a humming, it's quiet inside here ... very quiet indeed. As we descend the metallic walls of this profound and apparent secretive addition to The White House, I become increasingly aware of the heat making its unwelcomed return.

If I thought the upper level was hot, then this amply demonstrates my appreciation of the climate back there, compared to the stifling heat we now encounter.

The circular staircase leads to a metallic door, and this has a peculiar switch beside it. It's triangular in fashion and glowing a disconcerting electronic green.

"SHAGGY, I'LL BE EVER SO GOOD AND NOT PRESS IT THIS TIME. IT WILL, OF COURSE, REQUIRE A SCOOBY-SNACK."

I assume Jax is referring to the cartoon babble he's been watching, assigning me a name of one of the animated trolls.

"Listen, Bird-Brain, I'm not Shaggy and you'll have to forget the Scooby-Snacks. Just leave this to me. Now, move your fat butt aside and let me take a look." Surprisingly, he complies, allowing me access to the peculiar contraption. As I glide towards it, I beam my torch upon it and observe that it must be a sophisticated latch.

I push it, but the thing doesn't seem to have the same properties as a button. I then wave my hand across it, with equal futility.

"TRY SPEAKING INTO IT," Jax pipes up.

I slowly turn to face him, exasperated.

"And what exactly am I supposed to say?"

"PLEASE OPEN."

"Please Open, indeed!" I snort. "You utter numpty! Whatever it is, it appears to register a handprint, or something of that nature. The size of it betrays that fact."

"BUT WHY A TRIANGLE?"

"Because they felt like fashioning it so. How am I supposed to know that?"

"WHAT ARE WE TO DO?"

"There's only one thing for it," I decide, plucking out my sidearm and aiming it at the annoyance. "Blast the lock."

"YOU DO REALISE, DON'T YOU, THAT IF YOU DO THAT, WHOEVER RESIDES HERE WILL CONCLUDE INTRUSION?"

"No!" I sarcastically snort. "You don't say?"

"I DO. HERE, STAND BACK … I MIGHT BE ABLE TO SHIFT THE DOOR ASIDE, WITHOUT DAMAGING THE MECHANISM."

"How are you to get a grip?" I furiously demand. "The barrier is spotless."

He pushes me aside and presses his claws upon the metal.

"WITH IMMENSE SUCTION. I HAVE THE ABILITY OF MAKING THINGS STICK TO ME, IF YOU HAVEN'T ALREADY NOTICED."

"I have. Bird shit seems to be a favourite."

"METALLIC THINGS," he adds.

I am utterly incredulous as he grips the metal and forces the door open. Slowly, it slides aside, with us having a clear view of the innards.

Now this is where things get freaky! We are both taken aback to find a vast chamber, dimly lit, and of which seems to be pulsating.

But it is the thing located directly ahead of us which causes me to embarrassingly let out a pathetic gasp.

"WHAT IS A LAGOON DOING HERE?" Jax queries. "LOOK, IT'S SO HOT, IT'S ACTUALLY BUBBLING!"

It suddenly dawns on me that we are in serious trouble, and I experience a brief spell of nausea as I absorb the horrifying conclusion this discovery has afforded. The lagoon is clearly artificial, with a set of stone steps gracing the far right, and spans nearly thirty meters in circumference. The water within appears to be a liquified mud, which foams on the surface, giving the illusion of being alive. It churns and turns, and I see, to the far end of this sizzling pool, another door which is open.

"Switch off your torch, immediately!" I command, doing the very same. "From this moment on, we are to use absolute caution."

The dim lighting within the chamber affords us a degree of visibility as we gently, ever so gently, skirt around the lagoon.

To the far left, a rotary spit can be seen, and, to my alarm, I find numerous skeletons – feasibly trolls – sprawled out about it. The makeshift cooker offers another diabolical truth as I briskly put the pieces of the puzzle together.

"THE PRESIDENT MIGHT LIKE A SECRET DIP TO UNWIND FOR THE DAY."

Although he's whispering, I slap him across the chest.

"In mud? Are you braindead? And this heat is unbearable. Trolls would not bode well in it. And look at those skeletons! Do you think Madam President has a fetish for human flesh?"

I whip out a piece of equipment from my belt, aiming it directly ahead of us. It is a Motion Detector, to see if we have undesirable company beyond the door.

It is not responding, and I actually wonder whether the infernal heat is causing disruption? The bloody thing should work, and I curse it for being obstinate. I'm then overcome with a dreadful feeling of the sidearm being equally inert, and briskly check its readout.

It reads 'ARMED.' I am relieved, but only slightly.

In any case, my great lummox of a numpty is still operational, so that's a private blessing. He has his uses, if you consider the benefits of a tin opener.

We are now at the edge of the open door and I wave a hand at Jax to halt. I then listen, very intently, prior to peeking round the corner.

I can hear absolutely nothing. I actually lose my nerve, without the robot knowing, and hover back, pointing a finger at the door.

"You preview the innards and report back."

"WHY ME?"

"Because you said you like adventures. Go on, Scooby-Bloody-Doo … in you go!"

I ready my pistol and double check everything for a surprise attack. My personal forcefield is optimised and I feel supremely safeguarded as the great lummox pokes his head around the corner, intently gazing in.

"IT'S EMPTY," he reports. "BUT THERE'S SOMETHING OF INTEREST IN HERE. COME AND

TAKE A LOOK."

Before I can bark another order, he disappears within.

I lower my sidearm and hover inside the room. What confronts me is something which literally takes my breath away!

"SOMEONE'S BEEN BUSY!" Jax booms ahead of me. "VERY BUSY INDEED."

"Keep your bloody voice down!" I hiss.

There, right before us, is a spaceship. Or rather, a near-completed one. It looks to me as though it's been shabbily assembled, with makeshift metal jutting out above and below the oval-shaped construction. Its front is slightly raised, with three stumpy feet supporting the rear frame. I estimate it to be roughly 19 meters long and seven in width. The circular chamber it sits in is enormous, and there is a hatch which is currently open.

I am troubled by two things now. If it wasn't obvious before, it certainly is now: This is Baltazar's lair and it briskly becomes clear to me.

Madam President has been bargaining with the slippery serpent; evidently concealing and protecting him in exchange for ideas about cosmic weapons. No wonder NASA were so quick to conjure the Quantum-Pulse-Disintegrator-Gun.

These trolls are so treacherous, they'd form a partnership with brutes from across the stars, just to gain military ground. I am disgusted, but not surprised.

The second is even worse! I ascertain that it would be prudent for Baltazar to build a means of escape, should his hideout be uncovered. The fact that he's almost completed the current inactive pile of crap is a testament to his cunning, considering he trashed the last one. But, is he inside the thing, tweaking it for a sharp exit?

"Jax, be very careful," I whisper. "He might very well be inside," I urge, pointing at the open hatch.

I produce my recording equipment and begin to film the ship, hovering back to the main door and capturing the makeshift lagoon. I'm sure our illustrious Leader will be thrilled at the new discovery I've made. Indeed, the style of the Cruiser matches preferences with Draconian architecture in as much as it being totally bland.

I circle the craft with the camera, catching every detail I can muster, before reaching Jax who, mercifully, is stationary. I wonder if the next decisive course of action has confounded his simple little processors.

"BALTAZAR'S LAIR?" he queries.

"Indeed. But, what bothers me is that open hatch. Is he inside the ship?"

The robot shakes his head.

"NO. I CAN HEAR NOTHING STIRRING FROM WITHIN, OTHER THAN THE HUMMING OF THIS ROOM."

"He could be asleep?"

"IN THAT! ARE YOU KIDDING? THE LAGOON WOULD BE MUCH MORE PREFERABLE."

"Underwater?"

"WELL, HE MIGHT BE HOLDING HIS BREATH."

"Holding his breath, indeed!" I scoff. "Next, you'll be telling me he has toast and marmalade for breakfast."

"TOAST AND MARMALADE? WHAT IS THAT?"

"A troll's fancy."

"FANCY THAT!"

"Get up there and have a look!" I snap, furiously stabbing at the ship. "I'm tired of all this flummery and wish to exterminate the brute right now. I think I'm due a holiday after this bloody farce."

Jax is just about to set off when, quite suddenly, we hear a very disconcerting noise coming from the lagoon. We both turn back, startled, as a gurgling sound, accompanied by energetic bubbles, reach us.

Carefully, very carefully, I hover to the edge of the door and peek out. Jax does the same. His agile movements are not, for the moment, appreciated by me, as we observe something massive emerging from the murky water of the pool.

A central hump in the lagoon, rising like a formidable mountain, has rivers of filthy gunk running down it, and there is a great whoosh as it begins to clamber out.

It's Baltazar! I discreetly activate my camera again and film the gigantic monstrosity, raising his cumbersome backside into the open.

I don't believe I've ever felt shock in its rawest form, quite like I do now. I am literally in awe of the titanic dragon now snorting, growling, and mounting the incline. It's no wonder the Draconian Royal Family fear him, along with every other bugger refusing to seek him out.

I'm embarrassed to say I'm actually shaking! I'm trembling so much, I fear my personal equipment jiggling and possibly betraying our cover.

His back is to us and it appears we are, for the moment, undetected. As I momentarily study him, I am surprised at his swiftness, considering the enormous tonnage he's carrying, being so grossly overweight.

It is evident to me he's been snacking on trolls more briskly than first imagined, and that the accumulated fat has transformed him into a thing which could down the Royal Family in a single sitting, before savouring a sweet dish.

He snatches a rather large towel from a bland closet and promptly dries himself off, before tossing it aside and turning about to face us.

Our invisibility cloaks are optimised, though I dare not

move an inch, just in case Baltazar is psychic. If he shares the same traits as the dirty old tramps back in New York, we're history!

The infernal Baltazar, emerging from his makeshift lagoon

Mercifully, Jax is static and the unnerving silence, wafting through the subterranean chamber like an unwelcomed enemy, only adds to the tension. Like a Mexican standoff, we lock eyes and I wait with bated breath for him to turn, for me to slug a round of deadly photons into his scaly back. At the moment, it's too darned dangerous, considering he has lightning-speed reflexes, regardless of the immense load he's accumulated.

And then something utterly extraordinary happens! As the beast sniffs the air, he peers down at the side of his abdomen where, to my surprise, I notice a small metallic device located within the folds of his flab.

He turns it with one of his great hands and, within a few seconds, Baltazar is no more. Standing before us in his place is, of all things … the President of The United States! I am so bloody shocked, I swear I pass a fart!

The dolly bird then haughtily turns about and races out the chamber, up where we entered. She is so fast, I have no time to target her.

The electronic door Jax was forced to slide open closes behind her, leaving us standing momentarily stunned.

"I don't believe it!" I gasp, turning to face the robot. "I was wrong about the trolls. There I was, thinking Madam President had made a pact with the infernal Baltazar, in exchange for technological knowhow, when it was him all along! He's masquerading as the bloody President! However, to me, he looks like a man troll in drag and, pondering this, he should have visited Miss Universe first, prior to selecting a suitable model. He's evidently using some type of holographic replicator.

I gaze up at the stupid robot, waiting for a response.

"How that lolling, sorry ball of lard manages to park his oversized butt in one of those Limos, or sits on a troll-chair with guests for dinner, disguised as that, is quite beyond me."

Jax is not responding.

The dolly bird then haughtily turns about!

"Speak, you arrogant tin can!"

"I SUGGEST WE CONCENTRATE ON HIS CRAPPY SHIP, SABOTAGING A NUMBER OF KEY SYSTEMS WHICH MIGHT BLAST THE WRETCHED DRAGON TO SMITHEREENS, SHOULD HE ATTEMPT AN ESCAPE."

I am furious.

"He, I mean she, is not going anywhere anytime soon. She, I mean he, has control of this entire landmass, being one of the largest continents on this pitiful globe."

"THEN WHY BUILD THE CRAFT?"

"As a last resort," I clarify. "Do you really think that slippery toerag has any desire to leave, considering he's become leader of this wretched continent?"

"NEVER SAY NEVER!"

I lose my patience with the robot and wave him away.

"Do as you must, but be quick about it. I have need to return to the saucer and consult with High Command. I also need to conceive Baltazar's assassination."

I wait for him to nark me further, but am relieved he strolls off towards the ship. Resuming my glance on the lagoon and exit door ahead, I logically assume the infernal lizard will not return anytime soon, considering his swift departure.

Pondering this, I am utterly flabbergasted that such a titanic monster as he has so cunningly slipped into the human way.

I'm also bloody furious at the fact of losing my nerve in not taking a pot-shot at the dragon. I shan't relay that little annoyance to the Leader, informing him that this was strictly covert surveillance. I'll beef it up a bit, just to keep the old prune happy.

Although Baltazar must surely be occupied, I grow anxious for us to leave. I turn back and hiss within the open hatchway to the ship, with the robot evidently busy.

"Come on! I haven't got all day!"

He finally emerges, lumbering down the gangplank.

"ALL DONE."

I eagerly prepare to leave Baltazar's vile chamber.

"What did you do?"

"ENOUGH."

"Enough what?"

"JUST ENOUGH."

Again, I am irritated by his snotty attitude, but concentrate on us returning to the ship.

"Can you reopen that door up ahead?"

He casually observes it before responding.

"INDEED, I CAN. LEAVE THAT TO ME."

Thursday – 10th July 2027
Washington D.C.

Comfortably back within the saucer, I reflect over our departure of The White House and am assured we left it the way we found it. No one was present during our cautious withdrawal and I gather Baltazar was somewhere else, other than The Oval Office, when we nipped out.

It's just after midnight here, and all is quiet within the gardens of this rather tranquil part of the world. I see no reason to leave, considering we are securely camouflaged. Even if the mansion has detectors to sweep the lawns – which is a distinct possibility – we have not raised a single eyebrow.

I have engaged my Super-Snooper aboard the ship and am listening to the drivel some of the staff members are muttering within. As of yet, Baltazar (or should I say, Madam President) has not made a vocal appearance and I actually wonder if he/she has left the compound, on some tiresome official business?

No matter. With Jax deactivated beneath the saucer (until I require his services,) I am contentedly protected. Before I contact our illustrious Leader, I must first conceive a method of cornering Madam President, before pumping an endless round of deadly photons into her/him; filming the demise and then informing Galactic High Command, along with the Draconian Empire, that their worries are considered mute. With the old dragon eliminated, I can then expect a hefty reward, along with a very long holiday.

I then hear something very interesting on the Super-Snooper. I fiddle with the dial, just to crispen this new conversation up, and discover two male trolls having a disgruntled conversation.

"Yeah, she's making a public announcement here, this afternoon, with all the press and media glitz, outside and on the steps of The White House."

"Ah, shit … not another press conference!" the other troll gripes. "Why the heck couldn't she have told us earlier? Now that's my late-night screwed. I'll have to start organising the darned thing right now. I was looking forward to a beer and Netflix."

"You lazy old redneck! You're paid to serve her sweet little arse."

"Ah, just shut it! She's no dolly bird, anyhow. Looks more like a man if you ask me. I swear she's androgynous. No ring, no hubby … nothing!"

"I think she has her eye on you!"

"Yeah! I bet she has. It's a man, who fancies men, that's what I think. I'm hot stuff, but she, I mean he, can just forget it. I'm as straight as a ruler."

"The hell you are. I caught that glint in your eye when that new hunky, good-looking Captain arrived for a briefing, last week. You went all coy!"

"You're the one who went all coy!"

I can hardly believe my luck. The President, making a public announcement, here … and on the very steps of The White House. This will be the perfect opportunity for me to wipe out that overindulged, gluttonous greaseball once and for all, and I am excited at the prospect of the occasion being heavily crowded too. It'll weigh my opponent down, in terms of focus, whereby I can make a swift and calculated aim, before Baltazar goes 'Puff' … and right before the unsuspecting and gullible conference.

'Puff goes the dragon!'

I feel it high time I contact our illustrious Leader, to reveal all that I have discovered and to illuminate my intentions. Already, I have composed a plan of action and will need Jax for assistance. But, for now, I shall preen my good intentions to the old prune, back on Alpha Sector 3, and have him eating out of my hand.

I dial him up and wait. Eventually, after an annoying delay (intentional, I gather, to exemplify just how busy he is … which he isn't,) his ugly mug appears on the hologram before me and is, as usual, utterly unreadable.

"I hope it's worth my time, Taffy?"

"Your Imperial Highness," I humbly announced, giving him a brief head nod. "I bring promising news."

"Not good news, or settled news, and of what I come to expect?"

"Your Eminence, let me show you what we have discovered. I feel it will greatly interest you. And, I promise you, when this Earth day is out, Baltazar will be burnt toast. In any case, we're ahead of schedule."

I'm sure he's giving me the evil eye, but feel there's enough curiosity in him to warrant an extension to this conversation. He could just wave me away, or cut me off, but I don't think he's about to do that just yet.

"Go on …!"

He sounds really ticked off and my spirits momentarily drop.

"Watch this."

I activate the edited video I shot earlier, back in Baltazar's makeshift lair, and am pleased to notice him focusing on it. I know he loves his films, especially 'ALIEN' and 'THE THING.' He's also now started watching something called 'DALLAS,' and even went as far as wishing to have his own ranch built, along with owning a horse. He'd better not ask me to bring one of those bucking-snorters back with me, I can tell you. I can't even begin to envision old prune-face saddled on a thing like that. He certainly wouldn't appreciate it soiling his comely estate, along with having an insatiable desire for grass.

The movie plays out, with the infernal lizard transforming into Madam President, and I am watching bubblehead very intently. He appears extremely interested. When it concludes, he turns to face me.

"You can assure me that you'll have the traitor executed this day, and as it stands?"

"Without fail, magnificent Leader."

"So, I can prepare a statement, announcing the death of Baltazar?" he continued.

"Indeed."

"That I can submit it to the Draconian Royal Family, early tomorrow morning?" he stresses.

"Absolutely, Your Worship."

He pauses and closes in on the hologram.

"Just to remind you, Taffy; the Draconian Planet Decimator is en route to Earth and will orbit very soon. If you fail me, your actions will have dire consequences, not only for yourself, but for the entire human genus. Do I make myself clear?"

I nod, feeling a small lump growing in the back of my skinny-little throat.

"Crystal clear, Your Highness."

"You will do this for me?"

"Yes."

"To ultimately save the human beings and their quaint little world?"

"With pleasure."

"We cannot afford to strain relations with the Draconian Empire any further. It's taken me an infernal amount of time to build trust with them, as our combined forces can only strengthen our presence here, in this part of the galaxy. The Imperial Draconian himself favours our assistance and so, to that end, we shall not dent relations. We are making headway with them. We are building a bright future together. Is that categorically understood? Let me hear those golden words of yours, Taffy. Let me hear them, loud and clear ..."

"I shall not fail you, Supreme Ruler."

"Excellent. Your final transmission, when conveyed, shall confirm your noble courage in obliterating the reptile. When that happens, I shall reward you, very generously indeed. No slip-ups, Taffy ... no slip-ups!"

With that, the hologram instantly dissipates, and I am left visibly shaken. Added to the weight I now feel pressing down hard on my shoulders in saving planet bloody Earth, he's not disclosed where exactly the Draconian weapon will appear. You don't just zip up into space to find the thing as though by magic, as there's plenty of it to cover. If I had an inkling, I'd try and knock it out myself, feeling the lizards are taking things a tad too far. To exterminate an entire planet, just to be clean of a tyrant is, well – to put it frankly – disgusting. There is the hope that Baltazar's own weapon, affiliated with NASA, might do the job amicably, though I can't take that chance. It's just too vague.

I sensibly deduce that, considering I am ahead of schedule, we have time on our hands. Most certainly, I shan't contact old prune-face until, as I said, I've eradicated Baltazar.

I grow anxious and my previous enthusiasm is momentarily shattered. What if I slip-up? What if the entire thing goes completely wrong?

I'm sitting there, in the ship, mulling all this over in my head when, quite suddenly, something distracts me from outside. It's dark, though the garden spotlights betray a disconcerting sight. Knowing I am utterly undetectable to the staff and assumed President, the sight that greets my eyes is wholly disturbing.

There, in the grass, a number of meters from the ship, is Baltazar! Not the President, but the slippery lizard in his true form. He's crouched down in the grass, evidently waiting for something.

I am both anxious and hesitant, wondering just what it is the infernal thing is doing?

And then I see it. He swiftly catches something in one of his huge hands, before gobbling it whole.

Rabbits! The bloody thing has a fetish for rabbits! I gather trolls are just not enough to fill his bloated stomach, and conclude that this appetiser might resemble a dainty sweet he has come to appreciate.

I sit there, lofty and secure, and watch him shift … nabbing another.

He's crouched down in the grass!

I consider engaging the ship's weapons and targeting him there and then, but the revolving mechanism would generate sound, before I can blast him into tomorrow. Not only that, but the crafty old scallywag would deduce interplanetary intervention which would ruin the whole goddamn plan.

So, I just relax, in silence, and study him.

I am amazed as to how many rabbits he actually catches. Thirteen in total! He's now moving towards the water-feature and I guess he needs a drink after all that.

He sticks his short snout in there and thrashes it about, gorging the water in an upward fashion as it slides down his humungous gullet. He then dives into the pool, rolling about, with the fountain splashing off his glistening scales.

Another bath, no doubt … or the fact that any sign of water sends the croc into a blithering frenzy. After that, he vanishes … until I notice a skimpily clad female legging it back to The White House.

He's changed back again.

With the coming press conference inevitable, I sit back in my chair and contemplate the coming assassination.

I can't afford to fail this, or the whole bloody planet will be incinerated.

*　　*　　*

It is 3. O'clock in the afternoon when my ship detects groups of trolls, from the front of the mansion, assembling, and I rightly assume this to be the gathering of the Press Conference. I collect my sidearm, leave the saucer and activate Jax.

I inform him of my little plan.

"You must remain cloaked at all times," I remind him, haughtily staring up at the stupid lump. "When Madam President– I mean, Baltazar, starts her/his waffle, I'll hover just close enough, and then blast that dragon to kingdom come."

He absorbs everything without uttering a single word.

"If I miss, I guarantee you that slippery croc will head straight for his ship. Your job is to quietly pursue him and film the event. I'll wait in the saucer … to target his vessel and destroy it. I'll shoot my episode too."

"I AM SURE OUR EXULTANT LEADER WILL ENJOY THE FLICK, ONCE YOU'VE EDITED IT, CUTTING OUT THE BLOOPERS."

"We can't afford to make any of them. Just do as I command."

"AND WHAT IF HE DOESN'T FLEE TO THE SHIP?"

I am so tempted to just turn my sidearm on Jax, for his bloody matter-of-fact arrogance, but deem the stupid hunk of oil too important to lose at such a crucial time.

"I am hedging my bets he does just that, as he'll know he has intergalactic bounty hunters hot on his tail."

"HMMMMMMMMMM...!"

"Hmmmmmmmmmm!" I sarcastically refute. "Just get your sorry arse into gear and follow me. Everything hangs on this, Jax ... everything! If we fail, we'll all be toast. The Draconian Space Weapon is currently moving into this part of the galaxy and there's nothing we can do to stop it. Once we've killed the croc and offered proof, they'll suspend planetary extermination and have the wretched thing returned home."

This seems to do the trick and he actually salutes me.

"OKAY, BOSS ... I'M RIGHT WITH YOU."

"Good, and keep quiet."

*　　*　　*

Fortunate for us, the coming press conference is packed. I watch as Jax quietly skirts the curtain of trolls, standing at the rear and having a good view of the makeshift podium prepared for Madam President.

I position myself more inward, hovering about six meters above the presidential stand, where I have excellent range for the assassination. My sidearm is prepped and maximized for total obliteration, and I check the glowing indicators on its nippy console to ensure all is ready.

She has not turned up yet, and the television cameras facing the podium swing here and there as the crew set about testing their own equipment. Hanging high, I then turn to observe the sixty-or-so trolls; all eagerly anticipating their bogus leader's speech.

From this lofty position, I notice one of the male trolls surreptitiously heading for the bushes. I watch with curiosity, wondering what it is he's doing; until he unzips his hose and waters the plantation. I home in on him and note, as he's closing his zipper, a small patch of urine form on the fabric of his pants. He then beams a manly smile as he re-joins his comrades; his mannerisms depicting a Gillette moment. How embarrassing and primitive! He has evidently watched the testosteronised adverts, with it all happening on the day for the big man-of-men … busy, cool and being the centre of attention. I have examined a number of their commercials and cringed at a great many. If it weren't for my assignment, I'd blast old fish-fingers to atoms.

A female troll has a finger stuck up her nose, with a fat male eyeing her rear. I won't even report what I see happening there.

"Ladies and Gentlemen!" a fleshy female announces, mounting the podium and extending a hand towards the building's façade. I can see a figure approaching from the main door. "I give you, Madam President."

I peer down at the podium and watch as the tomboy leader arrives; smartly trimmed in a yellow blouse and matching shoes. Since when did Baltazar appreciate golden hues?

A thunderous applause follows, and the cameras begin to roll, with old dolly bird smiling and nodding to them.

I make certain Jax is recording the session, which he's mercifully doing.

"Good afternoon and thank you for attending," the President beams, appearing professional and to-the-point, with the fleshy female troll standing down and idolising her glorious leader. "Today, I have an announcement to make and feel, to make it more personal, you hear it straight from the horses' mouth."

I am not shaking this time, but carefully aim my weapon at her head; intently peering through the holographic target until the crosshairs match her cranium. However, I have to remind myself that the true Baltazar, expertly camouflaged as this influential troll, is vague in terms of focus, though I'm sure to kill him, nonetheless.

"As of this morning, I have decided to …!"

I have no interest in her apparent revelation and my patience wears thin in a single action that sends a searing bolt of light right down on her unworthy little head. It happens so fast, I am momentarily winded by the apparent ease of it all.

I hear the blast, screams and watch as the congregation quickly disperse, with the President... not dead!

There, in her place, is the true lizard himself!

There, in her place, is the true lizard himself; a titanic monster, furiously scanning the sky above and swiftly reaching for a pistol of his own. In the horror of the moment, I see his holographic projector burning on the floor beside him; sizzling and sparkling as it ends his flawless disguise.

I hit that! You're telling me, after all the goddamn preparations, I merely burn his bloody gadget to a cinder!

"Jesus Christ! The President's a bloody lizard!" someone hollers, racing and tripping across the lawn. "Shit – we're run by Demons!"

Baltazar can't see me, but he's as mad as hell, firing in every direction above; lifting his huge bulk and scanning the sky. He's looking for a possible clue in discerning a slight discrepancy in my invisibility shield. I am forced to abandon the area, due to retaliation, and barely miss a barrage of bolts.

I fire again and again, but just can't seem to hit him, due to evading his own vengeance. Knowing his actions are futile, Baltazar swiftly disengages the attack.

The cameras are unattended, but focused on the beast, and I wonder if they're still recording? People are clawing their way off the premises, including the guards and fish-fingers, and the infernal Baltazar suddenly lunges for a hapless male troll who has tumbled before him. He swiftly plucks him up.

"You're good for a snack!" he growls, racing into the building. "I've a long journey ahead."

I peer down at Jax.

"Now!" I shout, pointing at the mansion. "Get moving! Follow him!"

He races across the lawn while I, feeling my cloned heart beating ten to the dozen, return to the saucer. It is clear to me that Baltazar is preparing to leave planet Earth … and fast.

*　　*　　*

I barely arrive within the cockpit of the saucer when I receive a transmission from Jax. He's pursuing the dragon, though, and above the din of something mechanical and disconcertingly audible in the distance, I can barely hear him. The sound is winding up … like an engine of sorts.

"I'M IN BALTAZAR'S LAIR, PAST THE LAGOON AND WITHIN THE HANGAR OF HIS SHIP. HE'S BOARDED IT AND NOW POWERING UP. THE GANGPLANK IS RETRACTING. I SEE THE CEILING PARTING. WAIT! WHAT'S THAT? WHAT'S THAT? I CAN SEE THE SKY. YES – WELL, KNOCK ME DOWN WITH A FEATHER DUSTER – THE CEILING IS OPENING UP!"

"Where?" I anxiously demand, peering down at the grass outside for any possible change. "I see nothing! Are you recording this?"

The mechanical sound is now ear-splitting!

"Y..E..S. NOW … R..I…S…I…N……..G!"

Not one to take chances, I also power up my ship in readiness for pursuit. However, the saucer is shuddering, and this is not due to the engine; rather, the entire bloody area. The water-feature beyond, I notice, is violently juddering (with the fountain spraying everywhere) and the trees all about shake in a vibration that comes with a roar.

It's clear to me Jax is correct. Baltazar's ship is prepping to launch.

And then I see it! Like something from Thunderbirds (I must confess, I've watched a few episodes in the wee hours of the morning to kill apprehension,) Baltazar's bullet-shaped vessel rumbles up, just past the first set of trees ahead. I immediately retract the landing gear and engage thrust. Within a millisecond, I'm airborne.

I've lost communication with Jax, but that's a blessing. My only focus now is exclusively upon the ship. I MUST destroy it.

It's funny, you know, how the lizard's vessel appeared so pitiful when grounded, to now be transformed into a glimmering needle as it accelerates into the stratosphere. There's smoulder coming from the rear and, upon scrutiny, I realise the machine has an exhaust port; so he's possibly combined fossil fuel with his own technical knowhow, being that advanced resources are limited here on Earth.

Whatever he's done, his ship is brutally efficient. I actually take back the suggestion of it being crappy and wonder just what it is he's got tucked beneath its bonnet? Does he have Warp-Drive?

I crisscross the heavy downpour of fuel and begin to fire at it. My automated primary laser cannon tries to focus on the glimmering bullet, but it continually misses. I furiously disengage the computer and decide to take manual control.

"Bloody system!" I curse, firing at the ship. "Whoever

designed that needs shooting!"

I realise I'm recording the chase and that my vocals will be heard by High Command, when submitted. I'll edit that out later and if I catch the reptilian brute.

Now Baltazar's ship is glowing extremely bright. In fact, it's so sharp, it actually hurts my sensitive eyes. It's glowing like the Sun; the rumble of its engines shuddering my transparent canopy. I fire again … but miss!

"Shit!"

Suddenly, just as I prime my weapon for another assault, there follows an enormous flash, followed by a momentous bang. Even though I am sealed comfortably within the saucer, the blast rips through me as a terrific vibration, spinning my ship and causing it to momentarily lose control.

At first, I assume Baltazar's engaged Warp-Drive, until, that is, I see the ship disintegrating into a million shards. Huge chunks of it spin uncontrollably back down to the stratosphere, with space itself putting the dark smoke to shame. He's exploded, but I never hit him. I am certain I didn't get one lucky strike.

"He's dead!" I find myself repeating, unbelieving my good fortune. "The bloody lizard's dead!"

I have to pinch myself and wonder whether it's some kind of clever illusion, but trust the sensors of my ship enough to realise Baltazar has been destroyed. Gone. Finished. Caput!

The shards turn into silver glimmers of dust, to disappear from view altogether. I wait there, for a long time, to gauge what just transpired and, after a number of minutes, appreciate, with enormous gratitude, that my mission is finally and successfully accomplished. The feeling I now have, which is new to me, is of joy. I am buzzing with it and like it a lot.

After composing myself, I then descend to the planet … ready to collect Jax.

*　　*　　*

The robot is waiting in the grounds of The White House when I return, right where I last parked. With the saucer landed, I climb out and inform him of Baltazar's demise, replaying the holographic film.

"I never managed to actually hit the ship," I recount, frowning. "It's just beyond me. Perhaps it was due to dodgy wiring?"

"NO IT WASN'T," Jax informs, producing something from his back and handing it to me. "THIS CAUSED HIS ULTIMATE DESTRUCTION."

I peer down at a cylindrical piece of metal.

"What's this?"

"SOMETHING I TOOK FROM BALTAZAR'S SHIP WHEN WE VISITED HIS LAGOON, DURING YOUR RANT IN HAVING ME FINISH AS SWIFTLY AS POSSIBLE. I ADVISED THAT WE FIND A

WEAKNESS ... AND I DID!"

"But what is it?"

"HIS VERSION OF A SIMPLE FUSE."

I look incredulously at it and shake my head.

"You mean to tell me, this little thing here was enough to bring down that monster?"

"LITTLE THINGS MATTER. INCREDIBLE, ISN'T IT."

"Are you being sarcastic?"

"NOT AT ALL. WELL ... DO I GET ONE THEN?"

"One what?"

"A THANK YOU. IT, LIKE THE FUSE, IS A VERY SMALL THING, BUT OF WHICH HAS GREAT SIGNIFICANCE."

I am in two minds about it, and wonder how I can keep his trap shut when visiting the boss? If he blabs about his part in this assignment, I'd be looked upon in bad light.

However, he does, I begrudgingly contemplate, have a point.

"If I do this for you, will you promise to let me take full credit?"

"I HAVE NO EGO TO BRUISE ... SO, YES."

"Thank you."

To my immediate surprise, he briskly lumbers forward, grabs me by the waist and actually gives me an embarrassing hug.

"Ah, put me down you soppy great ninny!" I pitifully rebuff. "Come on ... show some masculinity about you."

He won't let me go.

"YOU KNOW, BOSS ... I'M SO HAPPY TO BE WITH YOU. AS I SAID, I LOVE ADVENTURES."

"Okay, okay ... I get it. I'm glad we've shared it together. Now, put me down."

He does as instructed and I actually feel a wave of compassion for the silly great brute. This growing feeling is disconcerting, but not altogether bad.

"So, shall we take a trip around this planet, after I've submitted the report? You and I can explore it together ... if you wish?"

"OH! YES PLEASE! ANOTHER QUEST ... ANOTHER ESCAPADE!"

He's hopping about with excitement and I actually laugh. I'm certain High Command will allow an extension here, considering the crap we've been through.

"Okay, I'll go and organize it. Wait here. And, Jax ..."

"YES?"

"Go talk to the birds. Rekindle our trust with them. They may just tell us where to find NASA."

"Why NASA?"

"To find that weapon the President put into effect. If we abolish that too, this chapter is closed. Our noble Leader would surely approve of that, I should think."

THE END

Scrapbook Section

The concept of the cover was, for me, extremely difficult to compose. Being an artist, I usually have an idea, though tried numerous designs, which, I'm afraid to say, didn't quite work.

However, Neil Geddes Ward, a professional artist, author and, more importantly, a good friend of mine, came up with a suggestion, along with a sketch.

My idea here, I felt, was too ambiguous, considering the characters are new and unknown.

The second attempt wasn't bad, but still, I felt, a little too chaotic. It would have stuck, had it not been for Neil.

So, I received an email from him, and was thrilled with his idea, having shown him the first proposal and of which he rightly expanded. Sometimes, simplicity is a good thing and, with that in mind, I set about using Zbrush, my preferred artistic tool, to revamp the cover under Neil's guidance.

He advised Taffy (the Grey) to be central, with the robot (Jax) behind. This way, they would act as a focal point, to draw in the eye and to make it appear attractive. So, I set about revising the characters, but could not, under my artistic limitations, get them synchronized in a way as to retain most of the detail. The Grey clashed with the robot, and vice versa.

The old saying goes, 'Never judge a book by its cover,' but the irony of that is, people do. It is the very selling tool which is used to draw potential customers in, in order to make a purchase. Of course, we all have different tastes, but the main consensus applied is to look attractive, and to do its very best in thrilling the reader.

It is interesting to note, when one is presented with challenges such as a cover, just how hard certain things can be. I was irritated at my limitations, though resolute in keeping with Neil's concept as a final piece of artwork.

So, I developed the modified draft, but again, there were problems!

The image was too dark and didn't appear to be as dramatic as I could get it. So, I told Neil I'd try again, and this time I gained results. It's funny, you know, how you just leave a problem for the next day – when you're fresh and eager – to find you are reinvigorated and prepared. A piece of advice for any problem you can't solve … just let it go and try another day. It does work!

Neil's concept

Neil Geddes Ward

I set about revising Taffy's posture, using the smashing Zbrush, in as much as portraying him physically holding his sidearm (not with it limply carried, or posed up,) angling him to the side. This method allowed a portion of the robot to be seen, though – and again – the clashing effect caused a problem. Neil advised blurring the background slightly, and set about creating this effect himself, which worked beautifully. Ironically, the simplicity of it was gained through a complex method of deduction and under Neil's guidance.

Neil also came up with the title of the book. First named, 'THE DIARY OF A GREY,' he decided on something more suitable and direct, that of 'I, GREY.'

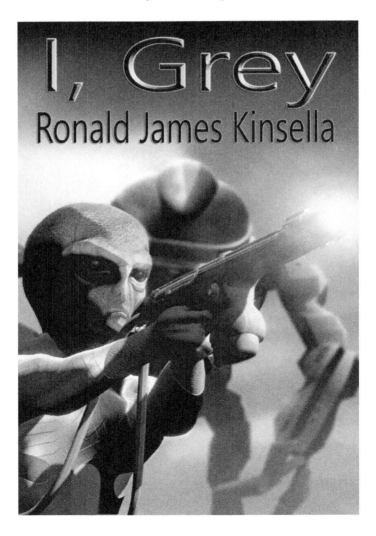

Printed in Great Britain
by Amazon